Serv

MW00411732

Vol. VI

By Cassie Wild and M.S. Parker

ISBN-13:978-1514399125

ISBN-10:1514399121

Table of Contents

Chapter 1

Aleena

Harsh, golden sunlight pierced my eyes and I immediately jerked upright.

Just as immediately, I regretted it.

Groaning, I sagged back on the bed and squinted up at the ceiling overhead. The ceiling wasn't mine. The slant was all wrong and the design...yeah, not mine. The windows allowing the sunlight to slant in and blind me? Not my windows.

Ergo, I wasn't in my room. Again.

Rolling my head to the side, I let my eye open a little more and saw the posts of the bed, a very familiar bed. I'd fallen asleep last night with Dominic wrapped around me.

It had been...intense. I shivered a little at the memory.

Forcing both eyes open, I looked around, but Dominic was already gone. There wasn't a clock—

Dominic wasn't much on having his time interrupted by menial things like, well, time. He was a punctual person, but when we stepped in here, the outside world ceased to exist.

I sighed. Unfortunately, the outside world kept moving forward and that meant I had to get out of bed, especially since I had the feeling that I was late. Judging by the angle of the sun, it was well after eight.

Dominic was probably already at the office. I grimaced. It was Monday and I should have been up and moving, heading out there with him so we could spend the first hour or so syncing his work and personal calendars. I'd have to call him and let him know that I was running a bit behind.

I rolled onto my back and winced. When we'd gotten back here Saturday night, after he'd taken my ass for the first time, he'd brought me to his room and told me to stay, saying he'd need me again. And he had. Again, and again. We'd spent almost all of yesterday in bed. Well, metaphorically at least, and my body was sore enough to prove it.

Moving gingerly, I looked around and saw that he had tidied up at some point, cleaning and putting away the toys he'd used. That didn't surprise me. He believed in taking care of his possessions.

And me.

My fingers lightly touched my neck where his collar had been all day yesterday. I missed it—that symbol of how I belonged to him. A reminder that I was his.

I smiled, remembering how he'd massaged out

the tension in my arms, shoulders and back after he'd released me from the ropes he'd used on me last night. He'd carried me to the bathroom and held me as we sat in the tub, his fingers coaxing me to a less intense, but still pleasurable, orgasm. Afterwards, he'd dried me off, slicked me all up and down with lotion, and carried me back to the bed, not letting me do a thing. I'd felt pampered and treasured. Completely adored.

After the weekend we'd had, I felt like I was starting to truly understand what it meant to be a Sub, and it was so much more than I'd ever imagined. So much deeper.

Then the guilt came back. I'd let him down. I hadn't trusted him.

The pictures flashed through my mind and I wanted to hit something. Preferably Penelope, although a wall would do, anything to empty myself of the frustration and anger building inside me.

"I should have trusted you more. I was wrong. Can you—"

My throat went tight as I remembered trying to explain to him—how I'd felt, what it had done to me to see those pictures. I should have trusted him, but it had hurt so much, brought up memories of the first boy I'd ever slept with. The only person besides Dominic I'd ever had sex with. That guy had used me. But I should have known that Dominic wasn't like that. It had been wrong of me, and I'd kept apologizing until he'd pulled me close and kissed me.

"It's over. We don't look back. You trust me. I

3

trust you."

Dominic had been angry though and I'd felt it Saturday night. But even then, I'd mostly felt his need. Now, I ached from it. Ached with it. More than the guilt, more than my own self-directed anger, and the anger I'd felt at Penelope, his need lingered.

Smiling, I slid a hand down my torso, imagining it was his mouth. There was no longer a part of me that he hadn't touched, hadn't claimed. I hadn't looked in the mirror yet this morning, but I knew there were marks on my neck, my breasts, my thighs. Marks made by his mouth. Bruises where his hands had gripped my hips so tightly. Then there were the invisible ones, the ones no one would see, but I would feel. The tender skin on my ass where he'd spanked me, used a flogger. The ache between my legs where he'd slammed into my pussy until I'd screamed. My ass, throbbing from his fingers and his magnificent cock.

My own fingers brushed over my clitoris and I gasped. It was already swollen and sensitive, or maybe it was just still that way, after being teased and tormented so wonderfully.

A lash of heat swelled through me and I bucked my hips. Eyes closed, I pictured he was here, with me. Again. Slowly, I circled my fingers over my clit. Then, quicker, faster. Dipping them inside, I flexed them, stretched them, opened them. My pussy was tight and it gripped me.

Moaning, I rolled over onto my belly and started to ride my hand. In my mind, it was Dominic.

He was under me.

Behind me.

Surrounding me.

He overwhelmed me and controlled me and dominated me in so many ways.

He owned me.

I gasped out his name as I climaxed.

***

I made short work of my shower and dressed. I needed to make up for lost time. I was ready in no time and dialed Dominic's cell to let him know I'd be on my way in just a few minutes. As soon as I found my other shoe.

He answered, but his voice was distracted.

"Ah...hi." My hand was damp as I gripped the phone. Instinctively, I knew something was wrong.

"Good morning, Aleena," he said quietly.

"Good morning." I looked out the window, staring outside into the park, my shoe forgotten. "Is everything okay?"

"It's..."

I heard it, the lie he was ready to voice. Then he blew out a breath. "Shit, I don't know. I'm in a meeting. It's...personal."

"Oh. I..." I frowned as I tried to remember what he'd had on his schedule for this morning. "I just wanted to let you know that I was running late this morning. Didn't want you to be worried. I'm sorry I overslept."

Dominic chuckled. It was a heady, intimate sound and it warmed the parts of me that had gone cool at the sound of his distant voice only seconds ago. Whatever was wrong, it wasn't about me. "I'm not sorry at all."

"Oh. Well...um. I'll be there soon." Where was my damn shoe?

"No." Although the tension didn't return to his voice, he still didn't sound quite himself. "Just work there today, okay?"

"Okay." I hesitated and then asked, "Are you alright, Dominic?"

"I will be. I'll see you later, Aleena."

The called ended before I had the chance to reply and I stood there, staring at my phone, trying to figure out what had happened.

It wasn't distance, I realized. He wasn't pushing me away and he wasn't angry.

He was upset. Cool, in control, Dominic Snow was upset enough to be distracted.

That scared the hell out of me.

Chapter 2

Dominic

I stared at the documentation covering the table. I leaned back, wishing I were in my office where I could pace. Lacing my hands behind my neck, I tried to still the restlessness burning inside me, although I knew it was a futile exercise.

"So do you want me to pursue this?"

I'd almost forgotten Stanley Kowalski was there even though he'd been the one to bring me the documents. He'd been waiting for me outside of *Trouver L'Amour* first thing this morning and had said he had something. We'd gone to a nearby diner to discuss matters. And we definitely had things to discuss.

He'd talked to my father.

I hadn't talked to my father in so long, I couldn't even recall the sound of his voice. Through the grapevine, I'd kept up with him to some extent. I knew he'd remarried five years ago. I knew he had two children. Two children who were biologically his. Two polite, well-behaved little Snows who were the exact opposite of me. His flesh and blood, ready to be molded into whatever he wanted them to be.

"What did you think of my father?" I asked Kowalski woodenly.

There was no immediate answer.

His face held no expression, his eyes carefully blank. He was good, I thought. Maybe I should hire him for any future investigative work I needed for the Winter Corporation. He just couldn't be ruffled. I appreciated that. But I had the feeling I'd surprised him.

"What did I think of him?" he asked, parroting my question back at me.

"Yes. What did you think of him?"

He angled his head, pondering the question. Then, he leaned forward. "If I give you my honest response, is it going to piss you off?"

"No." One corner of my mouth twitched.

"I think he's the biggest dick I've met in a very long time." Kowalski's smile was coolly polite, but his eyes gleamed. "I've worked with some of the *crème de la crème*, Mr. Snow. I've met assholes unlike anything you can imagine and your father takes the cake."

"I've met my share of assholes, Mr. Kowalski." A couple of faces flashed through my mind, not excluding a few men I'd had to deal with recently.

A faint smile curled his lips and he shrugged, a gesture far more casual than any he'd used so far. "Pardon me for being blunt here, but I grew up in the Bronx. It's a different world than what you know. You see things different. You're not quite as stiff in the neck as some of your peers, but even you see the world around you in a particular fashion. Your father, men like him? They see the world in two groups: their peers and everyone beneath them. It's one thing to deal with an asshole. It's another thing to deal with an asshole who doesn't even see you as a person."

I thought of how Aleena had said something similar regarding race and how people in my mother's social circle looked at her.

Kowalski brought my attention back by gesturing at the papers in front of me. "I need to know, would you like to continue with what I've uncovered, Mr. Snow?"

I looked back down at the papers. Even though there were several of them, they all dealt with the same thing. Adoptions in the state of New York the year I was born. Two of the pages were names and details of people who'd handled private adoptions...including a few black market adoptions.

Babies sold. Some without parental consent.

And I might have been one of them.

That was what my father had intimated to the PI.

My chest tightened. "I need to know."

***

An hour later, I was back in my office, standing at the window. I'd been standing there since I'd gotten back and my muscles were burning from being held in one position for so long, but I barely felt the pain. I'd mastered the art of not moving during my year in hell.

"Don't move a muscle until I give you permission. If you do, I'll know, and you'll be sorry."

It had been one of his favorite punishments for even the most minor infractions. Struggling when he wanted me to lie still. Not struggling when he wanted me to. Gagging when he shoved his cock down my throat. Making too much noise. Not making enough. It hadn't taken me long to realize that he'd just enjoyed punishing me.

I shook my head, hoping to get rid of his voice. Usually, the memories only came at night, but there were times when flashes came to me during the day, triggered by something specific. Today, I was punishing myself for being selfish.

I knew that what I was doing would hurt my mother. Did I really want the answers this badly? For all her faults, Jacqueline St. James-Snow was my mother. She might not have given birth to me, but she'd tried to do right by me. I'd had my doubts about searching for my birth parents, but after learning I might have been taken from my birth mother, I had to do it. Even if it hurt my mother. And I hated myself for it.

The phone rang and I ignored it. Three minutes later, it rang again.

My shoulders were rigid and fire licked up and down my back, but I still wouldn't move.

10

There was a knock at the door. When a soft voice said my name, I finally turned my head and that, in and of itself, was agony. People didn't understand the torture that could come from motionlessness unless they'd been subjected to it.

The new office manager stood there, a tentative look on her face. I couldn't remember her name. "What is it?" I snapped.

"I...ah...there's a Mr. Pence here to see you."

"If it's Mitchell Pence, call the cops," I said dismissively. I'd fired him. He'd been warned not to come back. I started to turn back to the window.

"It's his father," she said, her voice weak.

Slowly, I turned around. The fire licking my back worsened and then eased as I allowed myself to move. As though the movement had also lifted a veil from my emotions, I saw the anxiety in the woman's eyes.

"His father," I echoed. I immediately felt bad for snapping at her. None of this was her fault. Moving across the floor, I stood behind my desk.

"Yes, sir."

I nodded and then reached inside my desk, pulling out a contract. I softened my voice, hoping to repair the damage from my initial rudeness. "Have security find the feed from Mr. Pence's little...incident. They should know what I'm talking about."

Hopefully, Jacob Pence would prove to be smarter than his son.

As she went to shut the door, I spoke again, "Clear my schedule for the rest of the day. I'll be leaving after this."

I couldn't stay here. My temper was on a hair trigger. I'd practically bitten her head off when she'd only been doing her job.

I needed an outlet and there was one place I knew I could go.

***

Two hours later, I found myself in worse shape than before.

A new Domme, Maxime, stood on the Olympus stage. She wore an elegant corset of dark blue silk along with a skirt of white velvet. She looked like royalty and by the way she had her Sub kneeling at her feet when she was done, it seemed that the man with her thought the same. They were a unit, not just a couple of people who had hooked up for the day, and judging by the sighs when they left the stage, most of the people in the audience had appreciated the show. If my head had been anywhere close to normal, I might have appreciated the art with which she brought her Sub to the very edge.

But I was just as edgy as I'd been when I came in. I'd found no relief here.

A women in red body paint came to me, crawling on her hands and knees. She stopped in front of me and rubbed her cheek against my knee. "Can I pleasure you, Master?"

"No." It wasn't harsh, but it was final.

She made a low, disappointed sound and gazed up at me sadly before crawling away. That's when I recognized her eyes. She'd done this before, I realized. Maybe not wearing the red body paint, but I knew I'd been with her before. She'd probably even pleased me then, but I didn't remember her.

"I think you broke her heart."

There was no mistaking that voice. Deep and smooth, a warm bass that could sway juries and convict the hearts of the public, I looked up at District Attorney Jefferson Sinclair. He wasn't readily recognizable, unless somebody was really looking, and if they did, he'd be screwed. It was one thing for someone like me to be here. It was another thing entirely for Sinclair.

"Feel like living dangerously, Sinclair?" I asked. A prominent political figure like him being found in a place like Olympus was just asking to be a ruined political figure.

His teeth flashed white against his dark skin as he smiled. "I'm here...investigating."

That had my attention. "Investigating what?" I asked warily. I'd always gotten along with him, but that meant nothing when it came to political ambitions.

"That's not for you to know." He shrugged. "But you're in the clear so you don't need to worry." He nodded at the seat across from me. "Mind?"

Actually, I did. I wanted to be alone. But if he was sitting here, chances were nobody else would bother me. I preferred his company to another former conquest. I gestured. "Feel free."

He settled down, looking easy and comfortable in the elegant gloom of the club. Almost like he'd been there before and I wondered if he had. "Are you looking for somebody in particular?"

"If I am, would you be feeling helpful?"

I debated, then shrugged. I wasn't feeling particularly kind to a lot of people at the moment. Too many of the New York elite had done nothing but piss me off lately. My mother. My father. Penelope. Then I thought of Aleena and Kowalski, of Fawna and Molly. All people who knew what it meant to work hard, laugh hard and enjoy the things around them. Enjoy the people around them without thinking just how they might use that person. Then I studied Sinclair. I'd always admired him because, for a politician, he was surprisingly straightforward and honest. He played the game because he had to, but he truly believed in what he was doing.

"I might be feeling helpful," I said slowly.

"Depending on what I can offer in return?" he asked wryly. There was no cynicism in his voice. He simply knew what was expected in this world. Favors, as much as money and who you knew, made the world go around.

"No." I just shook my head and waited.

He looked nonplussed for a moment and then he slowly nodded. "I hear you're involved with somebody." Then he smiled, the grin going cagey. "I must say, Dominic. I caught sight of your personal assistant when you two were at a lunch with the director of the Met a couple of weeks ago. That smile of hers; I'd recognize it anywhere, even without the mask."

Shit. I'd forgotten that Sinclair had been one of the men who'd wanted to be fixed up with Aleena after her appearance at the masquerade ball. It felt like a million years had passed since then.

"At first, I thought you were a selfish son of a bitch, trying to keep a woman like that to yourself, but then I figured it out."

"There a point to this, Jefferson?" I asked, my tone bored despite the tension in my body.

"She got to you." He leaned forward slightly. "There's not a lot of things in this world that can make a man like you suddenly wake up and realize there's an entire world around him."

My jaw clenched and I glared at him.

"Aw, now. Don't go looking at me like that." Some of the polish left his voice and for a minute, he was just an amused man, grinning at me, almost laughing. "You're not a bad guy, Dominic. Not compared to some of those other high society dicks, but you're still one of them."

"You and I run in the same circles, Jefferson," I pointed out. "Those high society dicks helped you get elected."

"But I'm an outsider. Always will be." He shrugged. "I'm the black boy who comes from new money." He said the entire thing in the same derisive tone my mother would have used. "I graduated top of my class at Harvard, same as my dad. As a judge, he helped put away some of the worst scum this city has ever seen and he dealt with some of the worst scum you can imagine. But we've never been good enough to sit at the table with the rest of your lot, not good enough to drink from the same fountain as people like your mama."

"I'm not my mother," I bit off, leaning forward and glaring at him.

"No, and that's why I'm sitting here talking to you." He settled back, still smiling. "Your girlfriend...she *is* your girlfriend, isn't she?"

I blinked, staring at him. It wasn't just the abrupt change of topic that caught me off-guard. It was that word. Girlfriend. It brought to mind teenagers going to prom. A place in a relationship that was beyond friends, but nothing as serious as settling down.

Girlfriend didn't even touch on what Aleena had become to me.

For the first time, I admitted it out loud, "She's much more."

"I'll be damned," he murmured. Then he nodded. "Good for you."

The phrase struck me as strange. "Good for me?"

"Yeah. You're good people, Dominic. And I like her, your girlfriend who's much more than that." Then he laughed and stood. He looked around at the people below. The club was home to some of New York's elite. Debauched, yes. But elite. "She's real. You want to be happy? Find a woman who's real. That's what my dad told me before he died."

He turned to go.

"I thought you were looking for somebody," I

16

said to his back.

Jefferson glanced back at me and then nodded toward the stage. "I just found him."

I followed his gaze, caught sight of the man who'd just led a woman in a collar, on her hands and knees, up onto the raised platform.

"Show's not going to happen," he said as several people separated themselves from the crowd. Plain clothes cops, I was willing to bet. "Hope you won't be disappointed."

I ran my tongue across my teeth and then looked around as the cops approached the man on the stage. My vague sense of displeasure still lingered. I was disappointed. But not because of the show.

Shaking my head, I rose and turned to leave. When the aggravated voices rose to shouts of fury behind me, I didn't even pause. I didn't care who the man was or why he was being arrested. I didn't care that the show was canceled.

I only had one thing on my mind, one person, and she wasn't here.

The edginess, the restlessness, all of it was back, if it had ever left. The elegant depravity of Olympus seemed to mock me as I left the club behind, and I didn't give it a backwards glance. I didn't want to be there anymore.

Chapter 3

Aleena

I was smiling by the time Francisco left.

Aside from Fawna and Annette, he'd been the first to figure out things were more than just employer/employee between Dominic and I, though he hadn't said anything about it. I was a bit nervous about approaching him, wondering if he'd have a problem with the relationship.

When I'd told him I wanted to cook dinner for the two of us, he'd given me a long, thorough look and then he'd asked, "So are we talking a burger and fries kind of dinner, or something more?"

"More."

Now the penthouse was quiet and redolent with the spiced scent of the chicken dish Francisco had walked me through preparing. It had sounded incredibly complicated, but he'd laughed and assured me it wasn't. He'd been right. The meal, once I got past the fancy name and all the fancy descriptions and tools, was incredibly easy and my belly was grumbling.

It was also jumping.

Figuring it couldn't hurt, I cracked open the wine and had myself a glass as I waited. The alcohol took the edge off, but was hardly enough to relax me completely.

It was almost six and Dominic was rarely later than that. I paced around the expansive living room, trying to find something to engage my brain so I wouldn't think about the food, or the fact that I was nervous about seeing him.

I didn't know why I was nervous.

It wasn't like I hadn't seen him last night, or like he hadn't spent hours over the weekend either buried inside me, wrapped around me or standing over me as he administered various forms of seductive punishment. My hand automatically went to the place on my neck where he'd marked me. My toes curled into the thick pile of the imported rug under my feet and I tipped my head back as memory rolled through me.

The bed in the playroom had more accoutrements than I'd realized and some of them had very inventive uses. Dominic had chuckled at my wide-eyed astonishment and then he'd promised to show me some of the more unique toys he had at the house at the Hamptons.

I had no idea what to expect, but the very idea of it made me shiver in anticipation.

Need coiled tight and hot in my belly. I slid one hand up, cupping my left breast through the thin cotton of my sundress and the strapless bra I was wearing underneath. My nipples had already drawn tight and one tug had a pang echoing through my body, harsh and demanding. Wine splashed onto my fingers, but I didn't care. I pinched my nipple and imagined all of the wonderful things Dominic could do to it.

The door opened.

Lost in the moment, I turned my head and gazed at Dominic through half-lidded eyes. He stared at the hand that cupped my breast as he shut the door behind him. I gave my nipple one final, slow roll and then smiled at him over the wine glass before I took another sip.

I had one brief moment to process the flash in his eyes as he came toward me. Then, just as I went to squeeze my breast, he cupped my hand and did it for me, molding his hand to mine as his mouth came crushing down against my lips.

The wine glass fell to the rug and the remaining few drops of liquid splashed wet against my feet and lower legs.

He spun me around and I said his name, but he cupped his hand over my mouth.

"Shhh..." he said, his voice harsh, rasping.

I went quiet. The sweet, lazy daze of heat that had wrapped around me was gone, replaced by an inferno. The room tilted as he pushed me down, his hand still over my mouth. I caught myself on my hands, but sank to my elbows as he applied more pressure.

I felt the cool caress of air as he flipped up my

dress. The touch of his finger pulling aside my lace panties. Then he was inside me.

I gasped against his palm, shuddering and twisting as I tried to accommodate him. I wasn't ready. The light strokes I'd given my breasts had made me wet, but not wet enough. He tucked my butt against the cradle of his hips as he pulled out, then surged back in, deep and hard.

I moaned against his hand as his thrusts drove me face down on the floor, the weight of his body heavy on my back.

He bit the curve of my neck and then rasped against my ear, "Touch yourself, Aleena. I want you to come."

The angle was awful. He was huge and deep inside me, his upper thighs pinning mine close together. I had to force my hand between me and the floor, the carpet chafing painfully against my skin as he slammed into me, breath bursting from my lungs.

There was no finesse to this. I thought I'd felt his hunger before, but...no. No, I hadn't.

Not until now.

He wasn't in control and the realization sent a thrill through me.

"Touch yourself," he snarled again. "I want to feel you coming."

Pleasure burned me and I circled my clit with my fingers.

The hand muffling my moans moved away and he propped himself up enough that he was no longer crushing me even though his body still pinned mine to the floor. He nipped at my ear, the side of my neck, my shoulder.

"Tell me you're mine."

"I'm yours." I stroked faster, harder, feeling the heavy, furred sac of his balls slapping against me with each hard dig of his hips.

"Tell me you love me."

"I love you." The words seemed so small compared to what I felt for him. The intensity of it sometimes felt like it would overwhelm me. Shuddering, I twisted against him one more time and it brought of a rush of pleasure so all-encompassing, I thought it would end me.

His cock swelled.

I came and even as I felt myself clenching around him, he shouted my name, sheer uncontrolled desperation in his voice as he began to climax.

***

I sat up a few minutes later, my legs still too weak to hold me if I tried to stand. I wasn't thinking about that though. Seconds after he'd come, Dominic had pulled out, making my body jerk at the sudden loss. But that hadn't been as bad as seeing him drop to the floor, his eyes empty.

Worry overrode the pleasure I'd been feeling and I reached out to touch his cheek. Before I could, he caught my hand and stared at me. Suddenly, a look of abject horror flooded his features and he scrambled backwards so fast, it left my head spinning.

"Don't," he said, choking the word out.

"Dominic—"

"Don't!" This time, he shouted it and he was shaking. His eyes were wide and filled with self-loathing. "Fuck, Aleena...I just...how can you stand there like that after what I just did?"

I moved towards him slowly, not understanding. "I'm not sure what you're talking about, Dominic. What did you just do?"

"I threw you to the floor and..." He tripped over the words and as I watched, he backed into the wall, shaking his head the entire time. "I..."

"You didn't do anything I didn't want."

His eyes hardened and he gave me an icy stare. It was the stare I'd seen his mother give. Pretty impressive, really. "You like being thrown on the floor, somebody's hand silencing you, Aleena? I guess I've been topping you all wrong."

"Don't," I said firmly as I closed the distance between us. I thought I understood. "Don't you dare."

I reached out and put my hand on his cheek. When he tried to jerk away, I went with him. His eyes were wild, but I knew he wasn't seeing me when I leaned close to kiss his cheek, his jaw, his lips. His entire body was tense, shaking. His hands clenched into fists.

I got it now.

"You're not him." I spoke slowly and clearly so there'd be no mistake. "And I'm not you. I don't

24

mind playing rough, Dominic. And we both know if you'd been hurting me, really hurting me, you would have stopped."

He still didn't say anything. I slid my arms around him, ignoring the stiffness of his body. I pressed his head against my chest and stroked his hair, my heart breaking for him. I held him for several long minutes, and would have continued to do so if the timer from the stove hadn't chimed.

The first time, I just ignored it, but it did it again and he slowly stirred, like a man rousing from a deep sleep. He raised his head. "If that's food, you should take it out," he said, his voice hoarse. "Before it burns."

I looked down and saw that he was staring at me, his eyes haunted.

"I made you dinner," I told him softly.

An expression I couldn't quite recognize flickered across his face. His eyes bounced around for an endless time and then returned to me. Finally, he brushed a stray lock of hair from my face and nodded. "If you made me dinner, we should eat it."

I released him and got to my feet, keeping my face carefully blank as I felt his seed running down my leg. Anything that reminded him of what we'd done might set him off again. I held out a hand.

His gaze flicked to the spot on the floor.

"Dominic," I said his name gently, coaxing him back to me.

He looked at me and took my hand, letting me help him to his feet.

"Go get cleaned up and I'll get the food." I

released his hand and headed into the kitchen, ignoring the way my pussy was throbbing from how hard he'd driven into me. I felt his eyes on me as I disappeared around the corner and I wondered what had happened to him today.

***

I didn't say anything throughout dinner. I didn't want to disturb the peace, or his fragile state of mind. The silence wasn't uncomfortable between us, but there was a distance. It wasn't cold or angry, but I could tell that he was still distracted. What we'd done had taken his mind off of it for a short while, but he was thinking again.

Later, as we sat on the couch, I leaned against his chest, my fingers tracing patterns on his thigh. His arms were around me, solid and reassuring, but the motion of his thumb brushing across my knuckles was almost absent.

I wanted to ask. I needed to ask. I needed to know what was going on inside his head and what had him so grim, but I wasn't sure how to broach the subject. Maybe, I thought, he just needed to relax a bit more. Maybe in a less...aggressive way.

I sat up and turned towards him. He was already staring at me, his gaze troubled and intense.

I managed a lopsided smile that I was sure did nothing to hide the way my heart skipped a beat. Before I could second-guess myself, I asked, "Do you want to take a bath with me?"

"A bath?" He looked startled by the suggestion.

"Yeah." I reached up and lightly traced his lower lip with my fingertip. His mouth twitched when I did it and I laughed softly.

Dominic Snow, billionaire, control freak, was ticklish.

I repeated the caress and he caught my wrist, glowering at me. My heart gave another funny little leap.

"A bath," I said again. "You know, water in a tub. A hot, lazy bath." I put my free hand on his chest, reveling at the feel of the muscles beneath his shirt. My chest tightened. Damn, I loved his body. I gave myself a mental shake. I couldn't get distracted. I smiled at him. "Somebody had fun with me this weekend. My body's still kind of achy."

"Somebody, huh?" He slid his hand down my arm, around my shoulder and then up my spine, curving it around my neck. His skin was hot against mine. "Yeah. We can take a bath."

He leaned over and flipped up the arm on the couch. I watched as he punched in a few buttons then I rolled my eyes. He cocked his eyebrow in an unspoken question.

"It's too complicated to just get up and go to your room and run the water, huh?" I teased.

"The whole point of designing a home with things like a remote control bath is so you can start running the water from anywhere," he countered. He smiled, but it still didn't reach his eyes.

I shook my head. Both he and Fawna had shown

me the 'smart house' attributes when I moved in, but I had to be honest. I didn't see the point in poking a few buttons when it was just as easy, in my opinion, to walk to the bathroom and turn a knob. That way, I could make sure I had the temperature right. I didn't know if one hundred and two degrees would feel all that great unless I sat in it. Then again, I supposed this was another instance of trusting him to know what the right temperature would be.

He rose and held out a hand. I took it and we cut through the kitchen, stopping so he could get a glass of scotch while I poured more wine. Then we started toward the tub, the big, sunken one in his private bathroom.

My heart was in my throat the entire way.

We undressed ourselves in silence as the water stopped. I gestured towards the tub and he climbed in. I allowed myself to admire the long, lean lines of his body as he sat down, the water coming halfway to his chest. He looked at my body as I stepped into the tub, but he didn't meet my eyes. Tension turned his muscles to knots as I straddled his lap and looped my arms over his shoulder. Despite our nudity, his cock was soft beneath me. His hands held my hips as his eyes held mine and he sat there. Waiting.

I wished I didn't have to do this, that he'd just tell me what was wrong, but I knew it wasn't easy for him to talk about personal things. I needed to take the lead on this. It was my turn to take care of him.

Still, the words were harder to form than I'd thought. I forced myself to speak just as he did the same.

"I won't ever be that rough—"

"What's the matter—?"

We both stopped.

Looking away, I said, "Dominic, you've been rougher with me than that and I've *begged* for it. Why are you beating yourself up over this?"

He didn't answer and I started to suspect he wouldn't. His head bowed and he pressed his face against the valley between my breasts. I curled my arms around him, wishing I could protect him from the whole world. From anything. Everything. All things. But what had hurt him was his past and I couldn't fight that.

His breath was warm and soft against me when he spoke.

"He liked to hurt me, punish me if I disobeyed. Sometimes he wanted me to scream. One time, he told me to be quiet, but what he did hurt..." He took a shuddering breath. "It hurt so bad that I couldn't stop screaming, so he held his hand over my face so hard, so tight...I got sick. Choked on it. Passed out."

I dug my fingers into his hair, wishing it were possible for me to take away his horrific memories.

"When I came to, he was off in the corner. He just stared at me. Then he started asking me a bunch of questions. Like my name. Who I was. What year it was..." A shudder ran through him. "He'd had me for a while at that point, so I wasn't even sure. But I think..."

The words trailed off and he was silent for a while. I didn't speak, wanting him to finish on his own.

When he did begin again, his voice was a ragged, raspy sound, coming from low in his chest. "I think he scared himself. I think he almost killed me that time. He left that night. And..."

Now he lifted his head and stared at me. Fire burned in his eyes. Fire, fury. The remnants of fear.

"That was the night I escaped. He left in a hurry. Didn't secure his basement door as well as usual. I waited, kept thinking he'd be back and punish me for trying to run. Make me stand for hours without a break. Beat me. Torture me." He shook his head. "But I heard the car leave and I took a chance. Escaped." He looked away. "After what I did, you should escape...before I lose control and hurt you again." His voice was scathing, filled with something beyond loathing. It was hatred, all directed at himself.

"What he was doing to you wasn't rough sex, Dominic." I gripped the sides of his head, forcing him to look at me. Our eyes locked. "It was rape. Brutal, sadistic torture. What you do to me...it's nothing like that." I brushed my thumb across the side of his mouth. "You don't hurt me. You protect me. You take care of me."

His hands tightened on my hips, eyes darkening. He reached up and cupped my face between his hands, the touch gentle. Without taking his eyes off me, he pulled my face towards his until our mouths touched. Slowly, softly, he kissed me, so different from the frantic hunger I'd felt from him before.

When he finally broke the kiss, he moved so that

we were looking at each other again. "I think I'd go crazy if I lost you," he said quietly.

My heart lurched. He smoothed his hand down my back, settled it low on my hip. I leaned against him and felt my body relax.

That lasted all of two minutes.

"I went to the club today."

I jerked upright, barely missing hitting his chin with my head. "You *what*?"

A faint, but real, smile twitched his lips. "I went to Olympus."

I tensed. I knew what kind of club that was, what went on there. In theory anyway.

He brushed his thumb across my mouth, wetting my lips. "Relax, Aleena. I didn't go there to have sex. I haven't since I met you. I was just..."

He stopped and rested his head on the back of the tub. He said nothing for a long time, and I waited. My stomach twisted into knots, but I'd learned my lesson. I trusted him and I was going to give him the benefit of the doubt.

And then he was talking. Telling me about his meetings with a private investigator. Telling me about his mother—his *birth* mother. Telling me that he thought he just might have been stolen away from her. By the time he finished, I was gaping at him in blind shock.

"So I went." Dominic shrugged and looked away. Water lapped at his chest, at his arms. His eyes were hooded, staring off into nothingness. "I wanted to get out of my head and then I get there and all I could think about is you."

31

I'd been dealing with shock at what he'd said, but as soon as he mentioned the club, a stab of jealousy had gone through me. Now though...I leaned in and rested my head on his shoulder.

"All I can think about is you," he said again.

I curled my arms around his neck and kissed his ear.

I bit my lip, excitement and anxiety coiling in my stomach at the same time. Not wanting to lose my nerve, I said, "Maybe next time you feel like you need to go to the club, you can take me with you."

His body froze under mine. For a moment, he said absolutely nothing.

Finally, I looked up to see him staring at me with a shocked expression on his face. "Are you serious?"

I grinned. "Yes, sir."

Chapter 4

Dominic

I'd never been one to shy away from the hard shit. I might not enjoy it, but if it had to get done, then it had to get done.

Which explained why I had my morning cleared and drove myself to the elegant manor just nearly an hour out of the city to speak with Jacqueline St. James-Snow.

I loved my mother. She might not have given birth to me, but she had raised me. She had stood by me after my father turned his back. She had been there when the vast majority of her friends had whispered behind her back about all the *vile things that child must have done while he was...gone.*

Because of course it had been my fault. I'd been a wild kid, and had gotten what I'd deserved. They still hadn't found the man who'd destroyed me.

I'd spent a small fortune trying to track him down, but by the time the police had gotten involved, the evidence had been pretty much eliminated and I hadn't proved to be much use. My memories of that time were mercifully incomplete. Post-traumatic stress had turned my mind into a piece of Swiss cheese. What I did remember was bad enough. I didn't think I could survive remembering everything.

As for everyone else, it hadn't matter that he'd grabbed me, that he'd drugged me off and on for the better part of a year or that he'd held me down, beaten me, tortured and raped me, warped any part of me that might have been normal.

It would've been bad enough if I'd been a woman. People still would've blamed me. I knew how they talked. A girl wears a mini-skirt and she's just asking to be gang raped. As a fifteen year-old boy, I'd already been six feet tall and strong, evidence of the unspoken thought that men couldn't be victims.

You must've wanted it, twisted pervert.

Men can't be raped so stop lying.

Why didn't you fight back?

My mother had always been like that.

Not about me though. She'd stood up for me.

She loved me. I knew that. But after today, I didn't think she would like me very much, but I had to know the truth.

As I pulled up the twining, elegant curve of the drive, I stared up at the house where I'd grown up for bits and pieces of my life. Before the divorce, my family had spent summers and holidays here. After the...incident, Mom had wanted to keep me close so we'd stayed here. It hadn't bothered Dad that he didn't get to see me much.

I hadn't really cared much either, but after a few months of being at the house, I'd started going stir crazy. Mom, however, hadn't wanted to let me go. I knew she hadn't meant to make it into a prison, but she had.

Sometimes, when I came to visit, I wondered if a convicted man might've felt like this, taking a last gulp of free air as he walked toward a prison, knowing the doors would swing shut behind him, wondering if he'd ever breathe free air again. Logically, I *knew* I could leave anytime I wanted. But there were parts of me that just didn't understand logic.

I hated coming here.

Today it seemed even worse and I knew why. It was dread, plain and simple. I thought about what Kowalski had told me and I thought about the questions I had to ask my mother.

Those damn questions. I blew out a breath and shoved a hand through my hair, suddenly realizing I'd already clenched it into a fist.

How likely was it that she'd even answer me? Tell me anything? How likely was it that I'd learn anything?

Except perhaps the truth.

Not that she would intentionally tell me. I didn't expect that, not in a million years. She would look at me and she would lie. But I would see it. If she lied about the questions I had for her, I'd be able to tell. She had never been able to lie worth a damn. Truth or lie, though, the questions would hurt.

The final few yards lay between me and the

massive entryway and each step closer drew my muscles tighter and tighter. I realized some part of me had already known the truth. Not the details of course, but that I wasn't part of this world. Almost from the moment Kowalski had told me what he suspected was going on, I'd started to understand why I'd never fit in.

I wanted to run. I knew how to run away from ugliness. I'd been doing it for a long time. And when I couldn't run, I found other ways to deal. Alcohol and drugs as a teenager. Sex as an adult. Kinky, controlling sex. Work. My entire life had been about dealing.

The front door opened as I stood there, lost in thought, and I found myself staring into a familiar, ageless face.

George.

I nodded at the older man. Like with Maxwell, the driver who'd spent most of my teenage years chasing after me, I'd taken to George. I'd related to the butler better than I'd ever related to my parents. He'd been the one to tell me about being safe if I absolutely *had* to go out there and get crazy about the girls.

I'd been thirteen and he'd found me making out with some girl—I couldn't remember her name now—in the pool house in the middle of a cocktail party. He'd dragged me away from her and sat me down for an embarrassing talk about condoms, diseases, pregnancy and some other things that had turned my face red.

As a smile spread across his face, I did

something I'd never done. I moved in and hugged him. It was awkward, something I wasn't used to doing, but I found myself needing that quick, hard hug more than the handshake he'd always offered in the past.

That was when it hit me. That was why he'd started offering me the handshakes instead of a cordial nod. Formal as it was, he'd known I'd needed the contact.

He squeezed me back, just the same way I'd squeezed him, releasing a quick moment before I was going to. "Are you well, Master Dominic?"

There was no point in lying.

"It's all a matter of degrees," I told him with a tight smile. "And it's about to get worse. Where is she?"

He angled his head. "In her salon. Shall I bring refreshments?"

"No." I gave a grim shake of my head. If I tried to eat anything at the moment, I was afraid I'd be sick. "See to it that we're not interrupted."

George acknowledged my words with a quick dip of his head. "Of course."

My mother's salon faced out on the sprawling gardens of the estate. She sat on a sofa that was more elegant than comfortable and she reclined there like a queen holding court. A queen of a desolate kingdom, I thought.

When she saw me, she inclined her head. I thought I saw a smile in her eyes, but it was gone so fast, I couldn't be sure.

"How lovely to see you, Dominic."

37

"Mom." I remained where I was, near the doorway, ten feet away. It felt like an entire universe separated us. Tucking my hands into my pockets, I clenched my jaw. I didn't know what to say or how to start. When she went to rise, I held out a hand and blurted out, "Did you steal me?"

Okay, that was a little more blunt than I had planned.

Her eyes were wide. All the blood drained out of her face.

"I beg your pardon."

She sounded offended, but I'd seen something. A flicker in her eyes. Not...guilt, really. But something. Knowledge, maybe.

Taking a step forward, I forced my voice to stay calm. "You heard me. Did you steal me? Was I taken from some girl without her knowledge? Without her consent? Was I stolen?" I said the last three words slowly.

She laughed then. It was a nervous, fraudulent sound.

I was dazed, feeling like I had been cut adrift. I dropped down onto the chair behind me, but I was too far away and stumbled, off balance, almost falling onto my ass. I just barely managed to catch myself, hauling myself more firmly onto the seat. Then I just sat there and stared. She must have seen something on my face because her laughter faded and she jerked her eyes away.

"I hired a private investigator," I said. The flat, almost lifeless tone of my voice struck me as being out of place. There was a raging inferno of emotion within me, but none of it showed in my voice. I sounded dead.

My mother lifted a hand to her mouth. "But..." She stopped, then tried again, her voice shaking. "I don't understand. Haven't we done our best to take care of you? I've loved you the best I can."

"I know that." Pity welled inside me. Pity and misery. She was telling the truth. Jacqueline St. James-Snow had loved me the best that she'd been able. But it was her kind of love and it wasn't enough. Her idea of love was based on approval and living up to her set expectations.

I had always failed.

The fact that she'd twisted this around to be about her just showed how completely fucked up that had been.

"Look," I said and then stopped because I didn't even know what I wanted to say to her. After a moment, I shook my head. "I'm going to find the truth. I don't care if it takes a hundred years and every cent I have to my name. I am going to find out the truth."

Her gaze fell away, lingering on the hands she had knotted in her laps.

"It's up to you," I said. "But I've got a feeling I'm going to find out some ugly things. Are you going to tell me what you know and maybe, just maybe, come out of this with some dignity? Or am I going to have to find out everything on my own?"

A silence fell, one so heavy, so awful, I didn't know if she was going to say anything, but she did.

"You have to understand," she said, each word

halting and slow. "I never meant to hurt anybody. And if you were taken from somebody without her consent, I had no knowledge of it. That was never my intention. I did not ask for that and I did not want that."

I just nodded. So far, it seemed like she was telling the truth.

She didn't speak for such a long time, I started to wonder if she was done. I was beginning to get restless. I needed to move things along. Leaning forward, I prodded, "What did you want?"

She shrugged, a gesture that was so out of place, so casual, so not Jacqueline St. James that I didn't know what to make of it. A faint smile crossed her lips and she looked at me with more emotion in her eyes than I'd seen in twenty-eight years.

"I wanted you, Dominic. I wanted a baby, a child. Your father and I had tried for years to have a baby of our own, but we couldn't." She looked away. "*I* couldn't."

With the two children my father and his new, much younger, wife had, I'd figured that one out on my own, but this was the first time I'd heard her say it.

"We were approached by somebody who told us they could help. Maybe we couldn't have a biological child, but we could adopt. It could be quiet, completely private. Nobody had to know. They specialized in such matters. Placing children and families...people in...unique situations."

Unique situations. What the hell did that mean?

She laughed, and it was that nervous laugh

again.

"What are you talking about?" I had to fight not to yell now. That's strange emotionless tone was gone. I feel like my control was slipping fast. I needed answers before I lost it. "What unique situations?"

"Why, what do you think?" She stared at me with an expression that was almost pity. "Dominic, this man worked with families like ours. He found babies from..." Her words trailed away and I could see her struggling to find a way to explain this in a fashion that wouldn't infuriate me.

My stomach was churning. "Let me see if I can figure it out for myself," I said, my voice soft, almost polite. "Girls from rich families. Rich white girls who found themselves holding a little stick with two pink lines, right?"

The weak smile on her face told me I was right.

"He made the pregnancies go away," I continued.

"Yes." The word was soft.

My head was reeling. Rising, I moved over to the window. My muscles felt like they were locking down on me, so rigid, so tight. "Did the girls know?"

People who specialized in placing babies from problem pregnancies. The New York elite was compromised of some of the most conservative imaginable. Even now, a fifteen or sixteen year-old girl who ended up pregnant caused such a ripple of sensation, it was almost laughable. Except it wasn't funny.

A memory came to me. One of my father's old

friends had a daughter who was five or six years younger than me. I remembered her because she'd had a crush on me when I was a senior in high school.

About five years ago, rumors started that she was pregnant, fairly far along. Then she was in France. A few months later, she was back. And she wasn't pregnant.

I ran into her at a party over the holidays about a year later. She was young, had her whole life ahead of her. But she was just a shadow of herself. Haunted, almost gray by the misery that weighed her down. She was also a far cry away from the girl I remembered. She had been bright, happy, and now she was a shadow.

My mother was still fiddling with her skirt and I asked her again, "Did the girls know?"

"Dominic, you must understand—"

I shot up from the chair, glaring down at her. "Well, I don't! I don't understand. I don't understand anything. All I wanted to do was feel like I belonged somewhere. It was never here." She flinched at my words and I tried to soften my voice. "I know you love me. I know you tried. Solomon never did. He never cared and he certainly never tried. He couldn't make his disgust with me more obvious. It was almost a relief when he turned his back on me."

"You and I both."

At my mother's soft words, I lifted my head, studying her. She couldn't have caught me more off-guard if she had slapped me.

"Do you think that was easy?" She rose and moved to the small bar tucked in the corner. After she poured herself a glass of sherry, she tipped it in my direction. "Please pardon the rudeness. I realize it's early."

She took a sip, sighed, then tipped her head back.

I'd never seen her look more human.

"You can't know what that year did to me. But Solomon..." When she said my father's name, her face twisted in a scowl. "He acted like nothing had happened. Oh, he put on a good show when people asked about you, when the police came around, when it was expected of him. But when I was lying in bed at night, crying, grieving, worrying? He carried on, business as usual. He told me things sometimes just weren't meant to be and if it was that hard on me, we could always get another baby." She laughed again, but it sounded more like a sob this time. "As if you could be replaced."

I took a moment to process the words, to understand that my feelings of anger and abandonment towards my father were justified, that they weren't just in my head. Then I pushed it aside. I already knew what an asshole Solomon Snow was. I needed things I didn't know.

"I need to know how it worked."

Slowly, she lifted her head and gazed at me. After a moment, she nodded. "I don't know any details or specifics. It never occurred to me to ask. When they told me they could help me get a baby, a newborn, all I cared about was getting you."

"Okay." I nodded. If there was something illegal going on, they probably weren't going to let out a bunch of information, anyway. "Who were they, what did they want, how did it happen?"

She looked away. "It was easy. They wanted five hundred thousand dollars and I paid them. Not all of it up front, of course. I wasn't a fool. It was twenty percent up front. I offered to provide for medical care when it arose, but they said it wasn't necessary. The girl's family was to provide for the prenatal care. They just wanted to make sure the baby had a good home and would be loved and cared for." She took another sip of sherry, her eyes distant. She was smiling now. "Three weeks later, they brought you to me. I spoke with several people, but there was one man who seemed to be in charge. I gave him the rest of the money. He left." She glanced at me. "That was it. I never heard from them again."

"That was it? Just as easy as that? What about background checks, documentation, anything?" I'd heard of people going through more to adopt a pet.

My mother shrugged. "There were some documents. I was asked never to seek information on the birth parents. As it was never my intention to do so, that was easy enough to do."

She took a deep, shuddering sigh and then she rose. There was a credenza near the door and she went straight to it.

I was still struggling to figure out what to ask, how to get the information I knew she had to have. She had to know something. My mother was self-involved, self-absorbed, and selfish. But she wasn't stupid. Even as I was racking my brain, she wrote something down and then turned to me.

"This is the name I have. It's the only name." Then she looked down at the paper, folding it as she spoke. "Whatever you find out, please don't hate me. I only wanted a child, Dominic."

Chapter 5

Aleena

"Is she telling the truth?"

I sat across from Dominic and a piece of paper lay on the table between us. It was elegant, the palest of ivory and the handwriting on it was a sweeping, flowery scrawl.

Dominic hadn't answered yet. He was still staring at the name as though that alone would force it to reveal its secrets.

"Dominic?"

Slowly, he dragged his gaze away from the paper and looked at me.

He shrugged and rose from the table. I watched as he moved over to the bar and splashed some scotch into a glass. He paused, then shrugged and splashed in more. He tossed it back, grimaced and then I watched as he refilled the glass and tossed back the same healthy serving again.

When he went to repeat it a third time, I pushed back from the table. "You think getting wasted is going to help?"

"Can't hurt." He shrugged.

"No." I put my hand on his wrist and caught the bottle, tugged it away. He glared at me as I put the stopper back in the bottle and wrapped my arms around his neck. "If you need to lose yourself in vice, use me instead."

Heat flashed in his eyes. Then, with a heavy sigh, he tugged me against him, tucking my head under his chin. "Part of me wishes I'd never started looking into this," he said softly.

I tilted my head back and kissed his chin. "You want the truth. It's who you are."

His hands kneaded my waist and I arched closer, rubbing my body against his like a cat. He slid one hand down my back, bringing me flush against him. My body instantly responded to his, desire and heat flooding through me.

"Let me make you feel better," I said softly. "Let me take care of you."

I pressed against his chest, holding him at bay as I eased back. Watching him, I went to my knees. His eyes, hooded and dark, rested on my face. Without looking away from him, I loosened his belt and undid the buckle. I lowered the zipper and pulled him free. I wrapped my hand around the base of his thick shaft and watched as it swelled.

I leaned forward and took the head between my lips. He made a sound as I swirled my tongue around the tip. He fisted a hand in my hair, my name coming out as a growl.

I hummed in the back of my throat as I took him

deeper. He was only half-hard, so I was able to take all of him without any problem. He rolled his hips forward, forcing his cock deeper until he was bumping the back of my throat.

We fell into a rhythm as his cock grew, me swaying forward while he drove himself into my mouth. My breasts were full, heavy. My belly ached and my clit pulsed with each thrust of his cock against the back of my throat. I cupped his balls with one hand, balancing myself against his hip with the other hand.

He groaned and I felt his balls tighten. He was close. He fisted both his hands in my hair and pushed deep, deeper than he had before, holding himself steady.

"Relax, baby," he said, his voice ragged, panting as he held my head in place.

I fought not to gag, fought to relax the muscles in my throat as he came. My fingers flexed against his pants as I swallowed.

A few minutes later, he held me on the couch, his face buried in my hair. His arms tightened around me. "Thank you," he whispered.

"Any time." My voice sounded hoarse and I reached for my wine, taking another sip of it before I changed the subject. "What are you going to do?" I asked him, knowing I didn't need to elaborate as to what I was talking about.

"Give the name to Kowalski." His breath tickled my cheek as he spoke. "That's the investigator. I'll call him tomorrow."

"Call him now," I suggested. I angled my head

up and studied him. "You'll feel better once you do."

Resting my hand on his chest, I waited for him to respond.

Instead of saying anything, he shifted around, removing one arm from around my waist. From the corner of my eye, I could see him holding his phone. He used his thumb to pull up the contacts and scroll until he found a number. I listened to the one-sided conversation and then looked up when Dominic said, "Hold on. I'm not sure..." He glanced down at me. "When is my schedule free tomorrow?"

"You don't ask for much, do you? The sun, the moon, the stars..." I sighed and leaned forward, grabbing my own phone. After a moment, I found pretty much what I'd expected. "You're free after five-thirty."

"Thanks." He started talking to the investigator again. "How about six?" Then he fired off the address to the penthouse.

I blew out a breath and tried to figure out if having an investigator over to the house was something that required dinner...or just hors d'oeuvres. Or if it required my presence at all.

He hung up a few minutes later and wrapped both arms around me. As he rested his chin on my shoulder, he answered my unasked question. "I want you there tomorrow."

"I'll be there," I promised. I felt some of the tension ease from his body.

After a moment, he spoke again, "I don't think my mother knew—Jacqueline, I mean."

"She is your mother." I didn't let the personal

dislike of the woman show in my voice. She might be an ice-edged bitch, but she did love her son. She'd stood by him when others hadn't and she done what she could to make him safe, to make him feel safe after a terrible trauma. For that, I could put up with a lot of shit from her. "Whether she gave birth to you or not, she's loved you as her son for almost three decades, Dominic."

"I know." He kissed my shoulder. "I don't think she knew. She's manipulative. She can be cruel. She's very self-centered. But she's not self-destructive and while she's too caught up in her own worldview to see outside of it, she wouldn't be deliberately cruel, not like that."

I knew where he was going with this. "You don't think she could be party to stealing a child from his parents."

He was quiet for a long moment. Then he asked, "Am I being naïve?"

"No." I turned my face to his. He was so close, I could kiss him. So I did. "I think you're being a son."

***

Stanley Kowalski looked like the former cop Dominic had said he was. He had a thin, intelligent face and dark, shrewd eyes behind a pair of wire-rimmed glasses. I liked him almost immediately. He sat across from me and carefully selected a canapé from the tray Francisco had put together.

The chef had graciously agreed to come in and help put together some light fare for the evening. I'd told him I'd love him forever and he had laughed, told me that I already did. He wasn't wrong. The man was quickly becoming one of my favorite people.

"Is this something that's going to make me nauseated if I find out what's inside?" Kowalski asked, studying the colorful bit of food he held.

"It's cream cheese and shrimp." I grinned at him. "On a cracker. There's a fancier name for it, but that's basically all it is."

"Okay." He popped it into his mouth. "Good. Fancy name or no."

I laughed and gestured toward the tray. "I'm not much for goose liver or anything like that, so if I'm eating it, I try to make sure it's nothing revolting."

"A woman after my own heart." Kowalski selected another as Dominic moved to join us.

"She's my heart, so you'll have to find your own." He sat down next to me and took my hand.

For a moment, I was too flustered to breathe. He'd made statements to me about how much he cared about me, but he'd never said anything so casually, as if such a declaration was common knowledge.

I shot him a look, but he was studying Kowalski, completely unaware he'd just shaken the bedrock of my world. My hand shook as I reached for my wine and took a sip.

"I heard you got a hold of a name," Kowalski said.

Dominic nodded and passed over the sheet of paper. It was looking ragged, as though he'd handled it a great deal since yesterday.

The investigator read the name, lips pursed. It seemed to me that he took a lot of time reading that one, single name. Like he read it maybe five times over—or five hundred times. Finally, after what seemed like several minutes, he folded the slip of paper and held it up for Dominic's perusal. "May I keep this?"

Dominic shrugged.

He nodded and tucked it inside his jacket. "Does that man's name mean anything to you?"

"No." Dominic shook his head.

I leaned forward, drawing the investigator's gaze my way. "Should it?"

He shifted his attention to me, those shrewd, professor's eyes landing on my face with interest. "Well, that would depend." He spread his hands wide and said, "It's been a long time. News didn't travel then the way it did now, but people in certain areas heard."

"Heard what?"

We both spoke at the same time, leaning forward.

Kowalski pondered his response, appearing to give it a great deal of thought. Then, softly, he said, "There was a series of reports some years back. I'd just gotten my detective's shield, was working in vice. So I didn't hear everything. But it was a big scandal. Some twenty, twenty-five years ago. It all started with a woman. I'd have to look up her name, track down the cops involved...but she claimed she'd been pregnant, that she'd heard the baby crying. Then her mother told her the baby was born dead. She doesn't remember the next few days, says she thought she was drugged. She woke up in her parent's private villa in Italy. Took her two months to get back home." He paused, shook his head. "Big scandal. She went to the cops, fussed something awful because nobody believed her."

"Believed *what*?"

Kowalski smiled, but it was a tight smile. "That she believed her baby had been stolen. There was enough suspicion though, on the police department's side that they investigated...and a whole house of cards came tumbling down. They never could find the head man." He leaned forward, his eyes pinning Dominic. "Can you guess his name?"

Chapter 6

Aleena

Dominic's face was grim as he made his way through the kitchen and I could see him struggling with the news he'd gotten last night. It was in the way he focused on his coffee, his bagel, on anything and everything but me.

He wasn't trying to ignore me, I knew, but he was upset and when he was like that, he got restless. He paced as he ate, constantly moving and not talking. Not even looking at me.

I knew it was how he coped with things, but I still wished he wouldn't do that. I wanted him to let me in, to let me help him. Those were the kinds of things that we were still working on though and, for the moment, all I could do was be patient.

Still, there were things we needed to discuss that had nothing to do with Kowalski's news.

"I'm finalizing the plans with Annette for the house," I said, breaking the silence.

He nodded. "I saw them." Finally, a partial smile, albeit an absent one. "You put color in there,

Aleena."

"Do you have a problem with color?" I asked mildly.

His head jerked around to look at me, his eyes wide. "I didn't mean—"

I laughed. "I know you didn't. I just wanted to see if I could get your attention."

His eyes narrowed, but there was humor in them now. I felt some of the tension in my shoulders ease.

"You always have my attention." He took a step towards me. "Even if it doesn't seem like it, you're never far from my mind."

I shivered, then swallowed hard. I needed to get the conversation back on track before we ended up in the bedroom. Not that I didn't want that, but we needed to talk about the house. "Do you like it? The plans for the house, I mean."

"Yeah." He nodded slowly as though he hadn't given it much thought. "Actually, I do. I think I like it quite a bit."

"Good. I'll tell Annette to go ahead with it."

The silence came back, but it was less tense. After a few minutes, he sat down and I breathed an internal sigh of relief.

He gave me a thoughtful look over his coffee. "I looked at my schedule this morning."

I choked on my coffee. I coughed, grabbing a napkin to keep from dribbling coffee onto my good blouse. Eyes watering, I stared at him as I tried to restore the flow of oxygen to my brain. I tried to speak, but could only manage a croaking sound. I shook my head and grabbed my water, downing half of it. Dominic was watching me, the look on his face torn between amusement and concern.

Once I could breathe again, I managed to get out actual words. "I'm sorry. I could have sworn you said that you looked at your schedule."

He snorted and rolled his eyes. "Very funny. I do know how to look at it."

I squeezed my eyes shut, opened them, then did it again, playing it up in the hopes of keeping the good mood, even if it was at my own expense. "I wonder if pinching myself might work." Leaning forward, I stared at him hard and asked, "Who *are* you?"

His lips curved into that wicked grin that had my stomach, and other lower places, tightening.

"You keep that up and I won't tell you about the plans I had for tonight."

The low, smoky sound of his voice immediately erased any humor I felt. "Plans?"

"Yes." He lowered his coffee and braced his elbows on the surface of the table. "I made plans. Which would explain why I'd checked my schedule."

He cocked a brow, all but daring me to comment.

I held up a hand. "I'm all ears, Dominic."

"I was thinking we could go out tonight. For a short time, at least." He lifted a shoulder lazily, adjusted the shining cufflinks and glanced at the clock. "We have the interview with that magazine..." He paused, a distracted look on his face.

I supplied the name of the magazine and he

nodded.

Come on, come on...

He seemed to sense my impatience and I could all but *see* him dragging it out...check the cufflinks again...smooth down the drape of his shirt. Finally, he leaned back. "Would you like to go to Olympus tonight?"

My breath lodged in my lungs, super heating until it took everything I had just to keep my breathing normal. Curling my hands around the edge of the table that sat between us, I swallowed.

"Sure."

He could have been asking me out for coffee, a latte, a quick bite to eat at the corner deli.

But Olympus was a lot more than that. A *lot* more.

Casually, I reached for one of the bagels. I needed to do something. As I smeared cream cheese across it, I asked, "What should I wear?"

"That's up to you." He pushed back from the table. "Some people wear club clothes. Others are comfortable in jeans."

I frowned. "I doubt I'd be comfortable in either. So...it's basically whatever works for me, huh?"

"Yes." He came around to stand behind me, stroked a hand down my hair. He kissed my shoulder and then, quick as that, he was gone.

***

There were times when having an expanded bank account came in handy. Even with the extra money, for the most part, I'd stuck to the same sort of clothing styles I'd always worn, even if I did scale it up a little bit now and then. That didn't, however, include the business attire I had to wear for work. That was a different thing entirely and I had to accept that old adage that clothes made the man. Or, in my case, the woman.

But this wasn't a business thing. This was a *me* thing.

And I wasn't going to make it about labels. I wanted it to be about style, and for me, that meant one-of-a kind designs. I didn't really have the finances that allowed for shopping like this on a regular basis, but I did have enough to indulge for special occasions and if a trip to Olympus didn't qualify, then what did?

I rushed through everything I needed to do, getting it all done by one. I'd skipped lunch and had one of Dominic's drivers meet me at the door. I used them because Dominic wanted me to, but I refused to think of them as anything other than Dominic's drivers.

As I walked out, I was ready, credit card in hand and determined to find something that would absolutely blow Dominic's mind. I wanted to put a crack in his cool public demeanor. More than that though, I wanted to make him think about nothing but me for the night, wanted to make it so that the first thing he thought of when he needed release was me and not that damn club. And I wanted him to stop worrying about the investigation and what Kowalski might unearth, and what his mother had told him and all the ugliness we were going to find.

I knew we would find it too. Whenever I thought about it, my gut twisted with anxiety.

But tonight wasn't about that.

Tonight was just for us.

"Here you go, Miss Aleena."

I glanced out the window as Vincent came to a stop. He was Dominic's secondary driver, trading off with Maxwell, the driver who'd been with Dominic since childhood. I liked both men equally, though I'd always gotten the impression that Maxwell was a bit overprotective of Dominic. I was fine with that though. As much as he took care of everyone else, Dominic needed someone to look out for him.

Biting my lip, I glanced up toward the rearview mirror to see Vincent smiling at me. He was younger than Maxwell, but still a good decade older than Dominic.

"Ah...are you sure they aren't going to throw me out?"

He chuckled, his eyes shining and, a moment later, he was opening the door.

"You're Mr. Snow's lady. That's all you need to remember," he said, smiling at me. Then he gestured to the doors. "I called ahead. Spoke with the owner. She's already expecting you."

Mr. Snow's lady.

The words made me smile, blush. They also managed to steel my spine and I drew my shoulders back as I strode toward the doors. We were in an upscale area of Manhattan. Even the traffic seemed muted there and before I was within a couple feet of the door, someone was already rushing to open the door for me.

Within the first five minutes, I had a good idea how Cinderella must have felt when her fairy godmother showed up.

I had people rushing around me, bringing out dresses that ranged from the lewd to the lovely. I wanted something in between and while I had a hard time articulating that, the saleslady—a sweet-faced woman by the name of Jeanette—had no such problem. She stood there as I went through one dress after another, tapping her candy apple red lips and then smiled, waving everybody away.

"I saw the two of you," she said, her accent clearly French. "You and Dominic Snow at a party for his match-making business. You are..." She pursed her lips as she seemed to struggle for the word. "Hmmm. You are proper."

I frowned.

She laughed and waved a hand. "I may not have the good words, but you will see. You wait here."

She disappeared into the back of her store and emerged nearly twenty minutes later with two pieces of clothing in her hands. One was a black and white striped skirt, which I was ready to veto straightaway. The other was a simple, black top, strappy things falling from the top. No way. I'd look like a damned clown.

She saw the look on my face and waved aside the protests forming on my lips. "Hush!" Her brows lowered over her eyes as I opened my mouth again. "I say, *hush*! I know clothes."

I clamped my lips shut and hushed.

Thirty minutes later, I had to admit it. Jeanette knew clothes.

The skirt was the tightest thing I'd ever worn. She called it a hobble skirt. The black and white stripes that I'd feared would make me look whalish actually accented my curves, from my waist to my hips on down to my knees and my legs looked like they went on for miles. She'd given me a nude and black lace body brief. It was open-ended, meaning that under it, my crotch was completely bare, but it smoothed and sleeked and whittled me down in all the right places, so I wasn't about to complain.

The thought of Dominic having easy access to my pussy made my entire body flush. The blouse, if I could call it that, was black. It fit close and went up over my neck and shoulders in a series of straps and lines.

It looked like a cage. An elegant cage, but one nonetheless. Appropriate, I thought. I stood there for almost a full minute, staring at my reflection. The final result was rather startling. And I hadn't even done my hair or make-up.

"You need shoes," Jeanette announced.

"Hmmm," I said. It could have been agreement or disagreement or anything in between.

She laughed and came between me and the mirror. To my surprise, she pressed a smacking kiss to my right cheek then my left. "Shoes!" she said again, her voice firm. "An ensemble as ravishing as this needs the right shoes, *non*?"

I smiled. "Right."

She nodded. "Just so."

She snapped her fingers to the two women waiting behind me and fired off something in a spate of French so rapid, I couldn't possibly follow. They hustled me into the dressing room and hustled me out of the clothes, then they hustled out of the room with the clothes.

I grabbed the clothes I'd worn to work and quickly pulled them on, feeling strangely vulnerable being completely naked even though I was in a dressing room. As I adjusted my blouse, I sagged down onto the padded, plush chair and tried to think.

Well. I had a sexy outfit. That had been easier than I'd thought. The shoes couldn't be worse, right?

***

I'd been so fucking wrong.

Almost a half hour had passed and I was on the receiving end of the harsh, stony stare of Penelope Rittenour.

She didn't bodily bar the entrance of the posh shoes store where Jeanette had sent me, but she might as well have.

"They sell shoes that would suit your needs down on 5th Avenue. Saks. Bloomingdales." She paused, then laughed, the shrill, twittering sound grating on my nerves. "I realize you're paid well, but I doubt someone like you can afford this establishment."

I clenched a hand into a fist and told myself that an arrest for assault wouldn't be a good thing.

"Please excuse me," I said, moving to walk around her.

She didn't try to stop me, but she wasn't done yet either. She came after me, her steps lazy, her voice apathetic. She wasn't even talking to me now, really. She directed her words to the man she'd had carrying her bags. "Rupert, make sure you remember to get in touch with my assistant. I may have to find other arrangements," she said. "If they just let anybody shop here, I need to look elsewhere."

A shopkeeper came hurrying over and I automatically hunched my shoulders. The woman looked between us, from me to Penelope, giving me a once-over that stripped my confidence. When she rushed to Penelope's side, I gauged the distance between me and the door. It would be pointless to stick around.

"Ms. Rittenour, is there anything I can do for you?" The woman had one of those simpering voices I despised.

Penelope sniffed. "I doubt it. It seems you let just anybody in nowadays, Elinor. I doubt I can continue to give you my patron—"

Something inside me snapped. "Oh, shut *up*!" I shouted.

Her eyes went wide and so did Elinor's. I knew I

was about to make a scene, but my blood was boiling. I was tired of her.

"Are you really going to do this?" I demanded, sketching a line between me and her, feeling humiliated and out of place which I knew was exactly what Penelope had planned. I let it feed my anger. "Any time you see me, are you going to make sure everybody knows that I don't belong? Are you that pissed that Dominic chose me over you?"

"Chose?" She started to laugh. "As if he would ever—"

"But he did." I took a step toward her. "Dominic Snow would rather be with me, some nobody from Iowa, than with you and it pisses you off."

Elinor gave a soft gasp.

Penelope shot her a desperate look. "Are you going to let this woman speak to me this way?"

Before Elinor could answer, Vincent appeared at my side. I didn't know how long he'd been there. It could have been for five seconds or five minutes, but he was there now and that was what mattered.

"Ms. Davison." His voice was professional, as always.

I cleared my throat and fought the urge to dash the back of my hand under my nose. I wanted to cry and I wanted to scream and I wanted to hit something. But I forced myself to look at him with a placid face. "Yes, Vincent?"

He inclined his head. "Mr. Snow wanted me to escort you to Delacroix for more...superior service. They're expecting you. It seems they let just anyone into this establishment."

I flicked a look at Penelope and I found myself smiling. It wasn't a pleasant smile though. Harsh and brittle around the edges, sharp enough to cut. Inclining my head, I looked over at Vincent. "We should go then. There are only a few more hours before he gets home."

***

I had Cinderella's slightly naughty shoes and her slightly naughty dress, but instead of getting myself ready for my date tonight, I was staring outside.

It had started to rain on the way home and the melancholy landscape suited my mood.

Penelope had glowered at me the entire way out of the store and I could feel her dismissive sneer even now.

It had taken me a while to get it, but now I understood.

She didn't want Dominic. She didn't even care about him. All she wanted was his name, and I knew that if she knew some of the things tied to his name, she'd probably be mortified, but none of that mattered to her. She was the kind of woman who was used to getting what she wanted and she hated me because I had gotten it instead.

Shivering, I wrapped my arms around myself and rested my forehead against the window.

Sometimes, I wished I'd never left Iowa. Life had been easier there. Emptier, but easier. Maybe I hadn't fit in and some of the people there were as small-minded as Penelope, but at least they were used to me. No one made a scene every time I walked into a store.

I was so tired of it. I tried to find the excitement from earlier, but it was just gone.

Somewhere off in the apartment, I heard the front door open, but I didn't move. I couldn't find the energy to shove away from the glass or turn toward the door. I just wanted to stand there and do nothing. Think nothing. Be nothing. It was just easier that way. It always had been.

Chapter 7

Dominic

I rode up the elevator in a state of anticipation.

I hadn't been able to wait and had left the office an hour earlier than usual. I'd called Francisco and had been assured that dinner would still be ready when I arrived. Aleena and I would be able to take our time before heading to Olympus. My heart skipped a beat at the thought of taking her into the club. From the first moment I'd met her, I'd wanted her there with me. Now it was going to happen and I was equal parts terrified and excited. I didn't think I'd be able to bear it if it freaked her out.

At least she seemed like she was looking forward to going. Vincent had contacted me earlier and asked me where Aleena could find the best shoes, so I gathered she'd gone shopping. I was looking forward to seeing what she'd found. She had eclectic, but impeccable taste and more often than not, no matter what she was wearing, I wanted to peel her clothing away and fuck her senseless.

I went inside, desire burning, and then I stopped short.

Francisco met my eyes grimly and gave a pointed look toward Aleena's room.

Dinner was laid out, as I'd requested, but Aleena wasn't there. I wouldn't have thought much about that normally, assuming she was doing something until I got home, but the look on his face was telling.

"What's wrong?" I asked quietly.

Francisco looked down, his eyes going straight to his highly polished black boots. "Perhaps it would be better if you talked to her, Mr. Snow."

"I'm talking to you," I said.

Francisco blew out a rough breath and then he nodded, shoving away from the counter. He moved into the kitchen and I followed, watching as he quickly and expertly put together a salad. "She was out shopping," he said, his words as economical as his motions. "She visited several stores, bought several items. Then she ran into somebody you know." His gaze was thin and sharp. "Penelope Rittenour."

My heart plummeted. What had that bitch done? Slowly, I turned my head and followed the path of the stairs, upward toward where Aleena's rooms were.

"I don't know what happened," Francisco said quietly. He shook his head at my unasked question. "She won't say. But Vincent..." He sighed and then continued, "He said that...words were exchanged."

Penelope Rittenour was going to pay for

70

whatever she'd done to Aleena. But not now. Aleena needed me.

I gave a short nod and put my briefcase down before glancing at the table. "Will the meal hold?"

"I can put it away." He hesitated. "Or shall I wait?"

I almost said yes, that I wouldn't be long, but I had a feeling Aleena would need more than just an encouraging word and what she needed was more important than anything else. "Go ahead and put things away, then go home. We'll reheat if we have to."

The fact that he didn't protest my reheating the food told me more than anything how upset Aleena must have been.

A few short minutes later, I stood outside her door and knocked. She didn't answer right away, so I knocked again.

Finally, her voice came, low and rough. "Just a minute."

Like hell. I opened the door and went inside.

She stopped in the middle of the floor, her mouth twisting in a scowl as she glared at me. "Just a minute means I'm not ready," she pointed out as she dropped her gaze.

"I know." I moved toward her, not taking my eyes off of her. When I was close enough, I twisted my hand in her soft hair, tugging until she was staring up at me. "What happened?"

"Nothing."

The lie didn't show in her eyes, but I heard it, felt it. Dipping my head, I pressed my mouth to her lips. I kissed her softly, then pulled back just enough for me to speak. "What happened?" I asked again as I released her hair.

She sighed and shifted away, tucking her head into the crook of my neck. "It's nothing, Dominic. Stupid."

"Tell me anyway." I curved my arms around her and waited. Patience for something like this wasn't one of my strong points, but I would do whatever she needed, be what she needed.

She clung to me, hard and tight for another moment and then pulled away. Reluctantly, I let her go. A part of me wanted to order her to let me hold her, but I knew that wasn't the right way to handle this.

Her voice was flat. "I went shopping." She gave me a quick and brittle smile over her shoulder. "I wanted to knock you dead, you know?"

"You do that always."

The smooth gold of her cheeks flushed and I was happy to see a bit of happiness flash across her eyes.

"Anyway..." She fussed with her necklace. She rarely did it anymore, but when she was nervous or upset, those slim fingers would still sometimes seek out that delicate chain, as if asking for comfort from the grandmother who'd given it to her. "I'd found a dress—well, an outfit. A blouse and a skirt."

She lapsed back into silence, fingers moving back and forth across her necklace.

My curiosity got the best of me. "Can I see it?"

She frowned, then shrugged. "Okay." The word was devoid of emotion.

I followed her from her living room into her bedroom and saw the outfit laid on the bed. With one glance, I could see her in it. And see me taking her out of it.

"It looks a lot better on..." She ran her hand over the skirt, then picked it up, clutching it to her as she turned toward me. Several different emotions ran across her face. "I needed shoes. Vincent took me to a place that had been recommended by the shop owner. Penelope was in there and, of course, she started on me. I don't..."

Her hands tightened on the skirt and I waited to hear what that bitch had said to upset Aleena so badly. When Aleena's soft green eyes flew to mine, I didn't see hurt. Instead, the anger there burned through me.

"She doesn't even *love* you, dammit. She doesn't love you, but she hates that I have you and she doesn't. She could never make you happy, wouldn't even want to try."

Shock rarely stunned me into silence, but I found myself struggling for the words as I realized why she was so angry. I stared at her. This woman just might stun the hell out of me. Hell with that. She already had.

Aleena continued, eyes still flashing, "She pissed me off. Made a bunch of noise about how the store was going downhill if people like me were allowed in there." She picked up the blouse and laughed, the sound harsh. "I told her to shut up and you should've seen her face."

I wished I would have. Just the thought of it

73

would've made me smile if I hadn't been dreading what came next.

"Vincent came in before it got too bad. He must have radar because he mentioned how he'd spoken with you and how 'Mr. Snow' thought I'd be better off at a different store. The shopkeeper looked like she'd swallowed a lemon when she realized I wasn't some little match girl off the streets. So, I left. That's it." She held the two pieces up and looked at me, her eyes blazing as she changed the subject. "What do you think?"

I stood there, staring at her and feeling the weight of the love I felt for her washing over me. What had I done to deserve her?

"I think," I spoke slowly as I walked towards her. "That you are the most incredible woman I've ever known."

"Ah..." She blinked and then looked down at the outfit she held in front of her. "Well, if that's your reaction, I should go shopping—"

I caught her face and kissed her, slipping one arm around her to tug her up against me, trapping her clothes between us as I backed her up against her bed. The sheets were cotton, a high thread count but nothing like the silk I used. The bed was nice and sweet, and solely hers.

I'd never made love to her in here.

This was her space. Being with her in here would have felt like it would cross an unseen line. But those lines had been blurring for some time and lately, I couldn't even sense the lines.

The only thing I could sense was that I had to

touch her, had to kiss her, had to hold her.

I needed her.

Needed her in a way I'd never needed anyone before.

As I brushed a kiss across her lips, she sighed, my name escaping her in a whisper.

I swallowed the soft sound before kissing my way along the elegant line of her throat, easing her back until she was stretched out on the bed, staring up at me. She still clutched the clothes even as the robe she'd been wearing rode high on her thighs.

I crawled up to kneel across her hips, reaching for the belt and tugging it free, baring her to my eyes. Full breasts rose and fell with each breath, her nipples tight, begging for me to take them into my mouth. But I held back.

I put the blouse against her bare chest, smoothing it into place as though she was wearing it. She watched without a word as I smoothed it down, from her shoulders to her waist, pausing to mold the shape of her breasts through the material, circling her tight nipples. I watched as her pupils dilated and her lips parted. Her lashes fluttered. I dipped my head and kissed the line of her jaw, up to her ear.

"Beautiful."

"It would look better if I were wearing it," she said, the words breathless.

I reached up and traced her bottom lip. "I wasn't talking about the clothes."

Leaving the blouse in place, I reached over and picked up her skirt. I smoothed it over her hips, from her thighs to her knees. It would end just a few inches higher once she had it on, thanks to her amazing hips and ass. It would fit her like a glove, clinging to her and highlighting every beautiful curve, drawing the eye of every straight man in the club.

They would look at her and they would want her.

And she was *mine*.

I stretched out on top of her, needing to feel her body under mine. With the clothes crushed between us, I caught her mouth. I tugged on her hair, angling her lips toward mine. She opened for me and we shared one long kiss after another, exploring each other's mouths as if memorizing every inch. She caught my tongue between her teeth and bit down.

Fuck me.

Lust shot straight through me and I snarled, the urge to take her driving everything else from me.

I wanted her and I wanted her now.

I reached down and tore at my belt, one-handed, clawing it open and then doing the same with my button and zipper. As she sucked on my tongue, I somehow managed to free myself from my trousers and wrap my hand around my cock, groaning at the cool brush of air against my burning skin.

I needed her so badly.

I tossed her clothes aside, not caring where they landed, thinking only of burying myself in her wet heat. She opened her legs, her eyes boring into me as I pushed inside. She was impossibly tight around me and I tried to go slow. She lifted her hips to take me inside, shoving up to meet me, her hands tearing at

76

my shirt until she was able to dig her nails into flesh. I hissed. Her greed, her hunger matching mine, feeding mine.

Desperate, so desperate for her, I growled and withdrew. I held her there for a moment, then slammed into her, driving deeper.

More. I needed more. More of her. All of her. I needed her to be mine. Body, heart and soul.

And I knew what I needed to do.

The words burned inside me, a fire hotter than anything I'd ever known.

I tore my mouth from hers and she tried to bring me back, tried to kiss me.

Curving my hand against her jaw, my palm against the delicate skin of her throat, I stared into her eyes. I shook my head. I could feel the mad flutter of her pulse under my fingertips, feel each and every breath. She started to lift her head and I squeezed, waited until she relaxed back against the bed.

"Do you see me?" I demanded as I thrust into her.

"I see you." Her voice was rough, ragged. Raw. Her nails bit into my chest again and I knew I'd be marked. Knew that's what she wanted.

She wanted to mark me. Claim me. She was mine, but I was hers. I twisted my hips and drove deep inside her yet again. Her pussy clutched at me and the muscles that gripped my cock clenched tighter and tighter. I hissed out a breath, I pulled out and then surged deeper and held there, lodged so deep inside of her, I couldn't have gone any deeper.

There was only one thing I needed to do.

"I love you." I stared into her eyes as I said the words. The first time I'd ever said them to a woman. The first time I'd said the words to anybody in a very, very long time.

Her eyes went wide.

I pulled out and thrust deep, said the words again.

This time, she reached for me and I let her. She curled her hands around my neck, plunging her fingers into my hair. When she pulled my mouth to hers, I didn't resist. I let her kiss me and there was more than just hunger to her kiss this time. There was love and laughter and a promise of something I'd never known before.

We'd had sex before, and we'd made love before, but this was something different entirely. I couldn't put a name to it and I wasn't sure I wanted to. I wasn't sure I could handle it.

My climax welled up and I couldn't fight it, just as I couldn't fight the desperate way Aleena pushed me closer to it, her body moving with mine.

This wasn't about the need to control anything.

This was...claiming.

Me claiming her. Her accepting it.

Her claiming me. Me accepting it.

"I love you," she breathed as her body tightened around me. She arched up against me, crying out as she came.

"Mine," I ground out the word as I followed her.

I collapsed on her. Despite having come, my cock was still hard and throbbing. I wanted more, wanted a lot more, but my muscles had gone to putty. Her pussy fluttered around me, sending the most delicious sensations through me. Her body twitched underneath me and I rolled us until she was on top of me, our bodies still joined. I never wanted to leave her.

"Tell me again," she murmured, the words a bare whisper in the quiet room.

I slid my hand up her naked thigh and smiled. Her pretty new clothes were a twisted mess next to us and mine were in even worse shape. I was pretty sure she'd been grabbing her clothes instead of the bedspread. My pants were tangled around my knees, my shirt open. I was also pretty sure some of the buttons had been torn off.

And I didn't give a damn.

I said the words as firmly as I could manage, wanting there to be no mistake. "I love you."

She hummed under her breath, a low pleased sound. "I thought that was what you said."

A moment later, she stretched and rolled off of me, hissing as my cock slid out of her. She snuggled up against me and I groaned as that long, lazy movement had her rubbing up against me.

"I should move." She sighed. "Get up, clean up. Going to take me forever to get ready. I think we kind of trashed my clothes."

I wrapped my arm around her and kissed the top of her head. "We'll go another night. I think I just want to stay here, holding you tonight."

She didn't argue. She just wiggled closer and murmured, "I like the sound of that."

So did I.

Chapter 8

Dominic

I left the penthouse earlier than normal the next morning. It was Wednesday and since we normally went to the office together, I left Aleena a note. I'd send Vincent back to get her after I'd taken care of some business.

This wouldn't wait. I should have already done it, I knew, but I'd kept hoping the woman would show some of the intelligence I knew was buried inside that shallow, vapid brain.

The Rittenours, like so many of the families I'd known most of my life, owned a lovely house in the Hamptons, but they also owned a residence inside the city. Traveling to and from the city could be a nuisance, and having an apartment or townhouse, any kind of second residence, was common.

Penelope's townhouse was only a block away from the penthouse. It wasn't unusual for us to see each other on the street or bump into each other at a local restaurant or club. It wasn't any wonder I felt like I'd had her in my back pocket half my life.

Vincent came to a stop just outside the townhouse. "Keep the car running. This won't take long," I said.

I glanced at Vincent and I stopped with my hand on the door.

"She upset her," Vincent said.

The words struck me as out of place. We were friendly, Vincent and I, but not friends. Not like Maxwell, who'd been more like family than employee over the years. Suddenly, it hit me that, with as much as he'd been driving her around, Aleena might consider Vincent a friend and jealousy stirred inside me. It was stupid, but I wanted all of her tenderness, all of her heart. I wouldn't demand it though. Not from her. I wanted her love more than her obedience.

"Penelope upset Aleena, you mean."

Vincent nodded and glanced up at the townhouse. "Penelope made her angry at first, then she was just...sad, sir."

"I know." I climbed out of the car, but didn't shut the door. He didn't say anything, but I felt the need to make sure he knew why I was here. I bent over and met his eyes in the mirror for another moment. "I'm taking care of it. It shouldn't happen again. Not after today."

To my surprise, he climbed out of the car and studied me, but the look on his face wasn't that of an employee addressing his employer. His gaze was steady, as if taking a measure of me. I wasn't sure I liked it, but I waited to see what he planned to say.

82

"It will happen again," he said bluntly. "As long as she's dealing with sharks like Penelope Rittenour, it's going to happen."

I narrowed my eyes. "Vincent, you'd do well to remember your place."

"I know my place, sir." He nodded, stiffly. "But I care for Aleena."

Not Miss Davison now. Not Miss Aleena.

I scowled, possessiveness washing through me. She was mine.

Vincent's stance stiffened. "She's a friend, Mr. Snow. Nothing more. But she's a sweet woman. A kind one. If all you're doing is..." His face reddened. "There are plenty of woman who can offer you anything you need and they can handle the sharks. But Aleena..." His voice softened now. "Sir, she's a tough girl. Solid and smart and strong. She might even have a skin thick enough to withstand the attacks. But she doesn't deserve it, sir. If she's going to have to deal with people like that, I hope it's only because you plan on *staying* with her."

There was only one reason I gave him the truth. Only one reason I didn't fire him right there. It had nothing to do with the fact that he'd spent ten years working for me and it had everything to do with the fact that I could see the loyalty in his eyes. Loyalty to the woman I loved. Strange, I realized. That loyalty mattered to me now more than loyalty he should owe *me*.

"I love her," I said softly. "Does that help, Vincent?"

After a moment, he nodded. "Yes. Yes, Mr.

83

Snow, it does." He gave me a stiff nod. "I've overstepped my bounds and I apologize."

"No. You spoke your mind and shown me that you will always stand by her. That means a lot to me." I brushed an imaginary speck of lint from my shirt. "I think I'll reassign you, effective today. You're her driver now. Permanently. I'll find another driver to cover opposite Maxwell, but I want you with Aleena."

"Sir?" Vincent blinked, looking stunned.

"You're not fired," I said mildly. "Like you said, she'll end up around a lot of sharks and I'm not always with her. You know those people well enough because you've been around them for years. I'll expect you to watch out for her when I'm not able to. Are we clear?"

The stunned look left his eyes and slowly, he nodded.

"Excellent." I turned to look at the townhouse. "I want a list of names you think would be a good secondary driver for me. You've got seventy-two hours. Is it doable?"

"Of course, sir."

"Excellent." I started toward the townhouse. The brick walk way was patterned in a diamond design and my shoes rang on it hollowly as I strode up toward the door. The flowers were perfect, a brilliant spray of color and something in them made me want to sneeze. I stifled the urge and rang the doorbell. Only a few seconds passed before the door swung open.

The butler was young, polished and pretty.

Exactly the way Penelope liked them.

"Hello. Is Penelope available?" I asked.

He gave me a polite nod. "May I asked whom is calling?"

She'd gone for a Frenchman this time. Last summer, it had been an Italian.

"Dominic Snow." I checked my watch. "I've got ten minutes."

"Of course. Please come in, Mr. Snow."

As I stepped inside, a maid disappeared into a room, her head bowed so she wasn't looking at me. She wasn't young or pretty or polished—again, just as Penelope liked them. All the men were expected to be pictures of masculine perfection, but she deliberately hired women who were as physically flawed as she could find them. And then she spent a great deal of time mocking them. I'd seen it more than once. It had always been enough to turn my stomach, how cruel she could be, but it hadn't been until she'd started directing her barbs at Aleena that I'd felt compelled to say something.

I frowned. Had I really been any better than her or my mother? Just being silent? Well, that was over now. I was through just keeping my mouth shut. I was going to be a better man. For *her*.

"Ms. Rittenour needs a few moments, sir." The young blond stood in the doorway, an apologetic smile on his face. "She would love to see you, if you can wait a bit."

I checked my watch again. "Seven minutes."

He paled slightly. Then disappeared.

Penelope waited another five minutes. It didn't

85

surprise me. She wouldn't risk me getting impatient and leaving early, but she'd want to make me wait as long as possible.

There were any number of outcomes to this encounter, and none of them were going to end with us on pleasant terms, but considering everything she'd done, I didn't care.

Her heels clacked on the stairs, deliberately slow.

I could count an intake of breath between each languorous step and I wondered if she was doing the same thing, taking a breath before she descended. I smiled at the thought and continued to stare into the fireplace. If she wanted to play games, who was I to ruin the fun for her?

I'd be doing that soon enough.

I didn't know what would piss her off more, telling her that she's better back off with her digs at Aleena, or telling her that the services of *Trouver L'Amour* would no longer be available to her. She didn't particularly need the company, but Penelope didn't handle being dismissed well. As she'd proven more than once.

A delicate yawn behind me signified Penelope's entrance. I deliberated the empty hearth a few moments longer and then slowly turned to face her.

She'd had taken the time to groom herself, giving the appearance of artful disarray. A silk robe open over one shoulder, as if she'd recklessly pulled it on. Long, blonde hair hung loose and tousled down her back as if she'd just climbed out of bed, though she was wearing make-up. Oddly enough, she seemed to have forgotten her clothes in her hurry to dress. All she wore was a silk robe and the heels I'd heard on the steps. A pair of fuck-me shoes were visible, thanks to the long slit in her robe that ran high on her thigh.

Typical Penelope.

I smiled to myself, amused at the absurdity of it.

The smile must have caught her off guard, because her own lips curved up and she started toward me, a hand outstretched, as if we were friends. "Dominic, how good to see you. You'll have to excuse how I look. I wasn't expecting company."

I waved her comment off and effectively evaded having to respond to her outstretched fingers as I moved around the couch. "It's not a problem. This won't take long."

I chose to sit down in a narrow, wingback chair near the entryway, watching as she draped herself across the settee.

The robe's slit parted more. Much more and I'd be able to get an idea of her personal grooming habits. That was the last thing I wanted to see.

She rubbed one thigh against the other and chuckled. "Dominic, darling. You are always in a rush." Now her gaze turned sly. "I hope your...what's her name? Adriana? Leena? She's probably so grateful for your attention that rushing doesn't concern her. If she even notices."

If she'd meant to annoy me, she needed to do better than that. I laughed and hooked one ankle over my knee.

The amusement in her eyes faded and she glared

over her shoulder. "Andre!"

The blond appeared so fast, I knew he had to have been hovering just outside the door. "Mademoiselle?"

"Coffee, Andre. My head is pounding." She rubbed at her temple while the boy gazed at her adoringly.

Cynical amusement welled inside me. I wondered if she was fucking him yet.

She slanted a look at me. "Would you care for some coffee, Dominic? Andre is a wonder with it."

"No. I'm fine." I gave the boy a smile, but he didn't notice, eager to do his mistress' bidding. "How old is he, Penelope? Eighteen?"

"Nineteen, I think." She shrugged. "What does it matter?"

"Since you're fucking him, I'd hope he's at least legal."

The look on her face answered my unspoken question. "You're so crude. But of course he's *legal*." She fussed with the cuffs on her robe. "I never imagined you'd be concerned about my personal life, Dominic."

"I'm not." Giving her a hard look, I leaned forward. "But concerned about a boy who looks like he just might *be* a boy? Yes. That does bother me. Perhaps you can imagine why."

She straightened, swinging her legs around to the settee and giving me a cold look. "I don't bring children into my bed. You're the perverse one in the room, if you'd recall."

She sniffed just as Andre came back, a heavy

88

tray laden with a pot, a cup, cream, sugar and a small selection of pastries. His eyes lit up when Penelope smiled and even her casual dismissal didn't dim that pleasure. I almost felt sorry for him.

Once we were alone, I leaned forward. She sipped at the coffee Andre had prepared for her and studied me. "I assume you're here because your...Aleena...mentioned we'd bumped into each other," she said.

The smugness in her tone rubbed me raw, but I didn't let it show.

"Yes. It came up."

Her smile faded, bit by bit and I waited for it to fade altogether before I spoke again.

"We need to discuss a few things." I checked my watch, deliberately, before looking back at her. "First, I don't believe *Trouver L'Amour* is a good fit for you. Personally."

As her eyes narrowed and her mouth fell open, I continued to speak. "We will, of course, help you with finding a match for any engagements you've already prearranged, provided it's documented in your file, but beyond that, I think it's best that you find another company, should you still be searching for...true love."

"You arrogant—"

I cut her off. "Additionally, you need to be aware of some...personal matters."

Her jaw snapped shut and she crossed her arms, her expression childishly petulant.

"This cat and mouse game you're playing is going to stop. You will leave Aleena alone. If you don't..." I let my voice trail away. Up until that point, I had been smiling. Now the smile was gone and I showed her what lay behind the mask I wore for the world. "Let's just say that you don't want to find out what I'm capable of."

The nervous titter she gave raked down my back like nails across a chalkboard. "Really. Dominic, is all of this because your precious little secretary—"

"You damn well know her name is Aleena," I interrupted. I held up a hand when she opened her mouth. "Now listen to me, because you need to understand something. I'm in love with her. Got it? I love her. She's mine. And perhaps you haven't heard about how protective I am when it comes to what, and who, I consider mine."

Her scathing sneer twisted her face into something ugly. "In love? With that little bitch? She's only using you."

"Bitch? Really, Penelope?" I said, tossing her phrase back at her. "As to using me, that's more your speed than hers."

She came up from the settee, glaring at me. Her face was pale, two splotches of color riding high on her cheeks. Her eyes were wild.

"You are choosing that ni—that woman over me?!"

"There was never a choice." I shrugged, choosing to ignore the word I knew she'd intended to say. "I wanted Aleena from the first minute I saw her. You and I might come from the same world, but that never meant that I wanted you."

She shrieked and grabbed a small, crystal bowl

from the table, hurling it at me. It went wide, so I didn't even bother to duck. "Why? Because I won't kneel if you say kneel? I won't beg if you say beg? For fuck's sake, Dominic, is she that good at playing your sick little games?"

"Watch it," I said. Rising now, I caught her wrist before she could pick up the cup of coffee she'd barely touched. That might hurt. She wouldn't have to hit me with the cup for the splatter to sting like a bitch. "It wasn't that long ago when you wanted to be exactly where she is."

"That was before I realized what a sick, twisted pervert you are," she said, jerking back on her wrist.

I let her go.

Her gaze drifted down to my mouth and I saw the speculation, and the calculation, in her eyes. I wanted to laugh even as something cold twisted inside me. She wasn't the first woman to call me perverse only to decide she wanted to see how perverse I really was, first hand.

It wasn't a surprise when she lifted her hand and placed it on my chest. I caught her wrist and squeezed. It wasn't enough to hurt her, but it caught her attention.

"Don't." I kept my voice cold and flat, putting enough warning in my voice that she couldn't mistake what she heard.

"Oh," she said, her voice husky. "Is this how we start then?"

"No, this is how we end." I dropped her hand and scrubbed my palm against my pant leg. I stepped away from her. "I don't want you. I never did. I'm never going to."

She stared at me, uncertainty on her face. I wondered if this was the first time she'd ever been so thoroughly rejected.

"This is done," I said. "I don't give a damn what you say about me. I don't give a damn what you try to do to me. We both know there's only so much you can say and only so much you can do. You're not going to do much harm, if any."

Then I moved a little closer, watching with interest as she reached up and closed the neck of her robe. It looked like I was finally starting to get through to her.

"I can do a great deal of damage to you. To you, to your family, your business interest, to your charitable interests...to your reputation..." I let my voice trail off. "The damage you can do to me only goes so far. You care about what your high society friends think about you, but I stopped caring what people thought about me a long time ago. Strangely enough, people put down my eccentric ways to my traumatic youth." With a soft laugh, I continued, "Even my little perversions, as some people call them, aren't all that shocking to people. You'd be surprised at how many people you know share some of my little kinks." I leaned closer and murmured directly into her ear, "I wonder if they'd be as understanding about your fondness for barely legal lovers."

She flinched, then laughed, again, the sound nervous and frantic. "Dominic, you wouldn't..."

"Don't try to appeal to my sympathies. I don't

92

have any, and I certainly don't have any when it comes to you."

Her mouth trembled, then tightened as she looked at me and I had the feeling that for the first time in a long time, maybe ever, she really saw me. Penelope inclined her head and then asked woodenly, "What is it that you want?"

"I want you to leave Aleena alone. You are going to stay away from her. If you run into her shopping, you can say hi to her or you can look the other way. But you will not fuck with her." I checked my watch again. This was taking too long. "You will not sit around at your little parties and make snide conversation about her. You will not spread lies about her and you will not gossip about her." I waited a moment and then added, "Do we have an understanding?"

After a moment, she gave me a tight nod and I headed for the door.

"Dominic."

Pausing, I looked back at her. She stood there, shoulders slumped under her pretty silk robe, her hair hiding her face. After a moment, she looked back up at me and I saw a flicker of vulnerability in her eyes.

"Why?" she asked.

"Why what?"

"You said you loved her." Penelope fussed with the sleeve of her robe. "Why do you love her? You never gave me the time of day, but you love her. What does she have that I don't?"

Because it was the first time I'd ever seen

93

anything remotely human in her, I forced myself to soften my voice as I replied, "She cares about people, Penelope. If you've ever cared about anybody but yourself, you have never let it show."

Chapter 9

Aleena

A few days had passed and we still hadn't gone to Olympus.

As predicted, Dominic was already getting bored with *Trouver L'Amour* and had been exploring his next venture. He hadn't shared it with me yet, but I was pretty sure it had something to do with diamonds. I hadn't seen him much as his schedule had been packed full and I'd eaten alone every night. I wasn't upset since I knew it wasn't because he didn't want to be with me, but I still missed him.

I'd been dreaming about him when I was suddenly pulled from sleep by the sensation of being picked up. I made a sound as I struggled to orient myself.

"Shh, baby. You're sleeping with me now," he said softly. "Is that okay?"

I was too tired to make much of a response, but I did manage to nip at his neck and mumble, "What do you think?"

I thought he chuckled, but I wasn't sure.

I was asleep before we reached his room.

***

The next morning dawned...differently.

I wasn't in my bed.

And I was on my belly, facedown, with my hands bound behind me. The chill of metal and a faint *clink* when I went to move told me that Dominic had me handcuffed.

"There you are," he said, a smile in his voice.

"Hmmm...?" I struggled to clear my head.

He drew me onto my knees, guiding me and steadying me, allowing my body a chance to wake up as he positioned me.

His hand tangled in my hair and drew me upright while the other stroked up my middle, dragging the silk nightshirt I'd slept in up with it. "I seem to recall you biting me last night, Aleena. Do you recall that?"

His fingers plucked at my left nipple.

A few more cobwebs fell away and I shivered. "No."

Then I stopped and thought. Had I bitten him?

Suddenly, I was back on my hands and knees, gasping as he spanked me. Two hard, solid smacks to either cheek. I was definitely awake now.

He brought me back upright, slow, using his fist in my hair. Once he had me flush against his chest, he asked again. "Did you bite?"

I whimpered and then said, "I don't know. Maybe? I was half asleep. I don't remember."

"Good girl." He cupped my breast again and rewarded me with a quick twist of my nipple that sent an arrow of pleasure straight down my core,

96

licking at my pussy. His hand slid down my body and I shivered when he started to stroke me through my panties. "You're wearing underwear, Aleena."

"I'm sorry, sir."

He laughed. "Do you want to stop wearing underwear?" he asked, amusement in his voice. "Be honest."

I squirmed and then answered, "No."

"Then don't lie. Besides..." He nudged me down again. When I had my face pressed to the mattress, he started to tug on my panties, dragging the silk so that it was rubbing against me, over my clit, between the cheeks of my ass. "If you wear it, I get to play with it. Get to feel how wet I make you." He squeezed my ass. "Take them off of you."

I shuddered.

"We need to talk about you biting me. Was that the appropriate way to say hello?" he asked.

"I..." My mind struggled for an answer, because dammit, sometimes I just wanted to bite him. Besides, he bit me too, and I knew he liked it as much as I did.

I took too long to answer and his hand came down on my ass again. I yelped and instinctively responded. "No. No, sir!"

"Then why did you do it?" He spanked me again before I even had a chance to respond.

I gasped and lifted my butt, arousal twisting me into a hot, tight knot.

"You woke me up, sir. I wasn't thinking."

"Aleena..." There was a warning in his voice.

I made myself be completely honest. "Because I

wanted to, sir. I like biting you."

"Why?" The hitch in his voice encouraged me to tell the truth.

"Because I like marking you." His hand flexed on my ass. "You're mine."

"Fuck." The word came out in a groan. He leaned down so that his mouth was pressed against my ear. "I am yours. And you're mine." He straightened and delivered two sharp stinging blows to my ass. "But I think you forgot who's in charge, and I really should punish you for that." He cupped my ass and then trailed his fingers over my hot, sensitive skin. "I'm wondering what I should do."

I was tempted to wiggle my butt, but I was afraid if I did I would give him the wrong sort of idea. I wanted him, but I also wanted to be able to sit today. But then he smoothed his hand down the curve of my hip and I couldn't help but wiggle, then sigh.

The sigh turned into a wail because he was suddenly inside me, deep and hard and fast. So hard and fast, it hurt. It bruised. I was wet, but not wet enough. Too tight. But it was a delicious pain and I arched my back to take him deeper. I wanted all of him.

When he was completely wedged within me, he placed his hand at the small of my back. "Be still, Aleena. Be still now."

I moaned as he closed his hand around the cuffs that held my hands, and then he started to move. I gasped as he thrust into me and instinctively began to roll my hips, needing to move with him.

Immediately he stopped.

"I said be still."

His cock pulsed inside me, throbbed. I could feel the orgasm hovering at the very core of me, but he wouldn't fucking move. He held still, locked within, just waiting.

"What are you supposed to say, Aleena?"

"Yes, sir."

I nearly sobbed in relief as he started to move again. I held there, focusing everything I had on not moving, on being still, just so he wouldn't stop.

"That's a good girl." His voice was low and ragged.

I jumped as his hand came down on my ass. Hard.

Immediately, he went still again. "Be *still*."

"I'm sorry." My voice broke as I said it. I was so close. My muscles were quivering, my clit throbbing. It was agony and ecstasy and I wasn't sure I could take anymore. "I'm sorry, sir. Please forgive me, sir."

"Be still."

This time, when he began to move against me hard and fast, he spanked me, alternating thrusts and sharp smacks on either cheek. Thrust in, spank. Pull out, spank. Each time, it seemed he went deeper and the blows became harder until my skin burned and I was nothing more than a burning, aching mass of need.

And I held still.

My climax was growing, swelling, a massive thing, so huge, I thought it might tear me apart.

"Please," I started to beg, tears streaming down my face at the overload of sensations racing through

99

me. "Please, sir, please let me come. Please, *please, please!*"

He bent low over me. Brushing my hair back from my ear, he said roughly, "Come for me, Aleena. Come now."

I came for him. I'd always come for him.

As my climax crashed over me, I felt his hips jerk, losing his rhythm. Losing control. He said my name as he came and my final thought before nearly passing out was that I was going to like waking up next to him.

***

He woke me with sex and left me with a promise.

I was slumped over the breakfast bar in the kitchen when he came in nearly an hour later and pressed a kiss to my neck. "We're going out tonight. Wear those pretty clothes I haven't gotten to see you in yet. They've been washed and pressed."

"Umm." I smiled at him, but that was about all I had the energy for.

He chuckled and kissed my cheek. I tried to work up the brain power to make words. But again, *umm* was all I could do.

He left me sitting there and I dropped my head onto the surface of the bar, thought about the pretty clothes he'd mentioned.

We were going out.

Going out...

I jerked my head up, lethargy gone under a rush of panic.

Going out?

As in...*out*?

Olympus.

***

Our regular car wasn't waiting when we stepped out of the penthouse. In its place was a long, sleek stretch limo.

I looked from the car to Dominic. "What's this?"

"A surprise. I thought you'd enjoy a little bit of luxury."

Running my tongue across my teeth, I looked up at the penthouse and then back at him. "Dominic, I live with more luxury than I know how to handle."

He traced his finger down my cheek and that light touch made me shiver. "I like to spoil you. Indulge me."

"Indulge you?" I shook my head and smiled. "The last thing you need is to be indulged." But I let him assist me into the back of the car. The driver remained by the door, making no move to help me. Even though I didn't know his name, I knew he must've been with Dominic long enough to know better.

Dominic had this thing about being the one to help me in and out when we went anywhere. The possessiveness of it thrilled me to the bone, even if it did feel silly sometimes. It wasn't like I didn't know how to open a door. Although, today I needed the help. The narrow fit of my skirt made it almost impossible to climb gracefully in and out of a car, even with help.

The drive through the city was an exercise in elegant efficiency. Before I'd met Dominic, driving around in a car had just been that...driving around in a car. I had driven myself from Iowa to New York, but the first thing I'd done once I'd gotten here was sell my car.

Driving in New York was for taxi drivers and the people who could afford to actually park their cars. Also for the crazy people who don't mind the insane driving and the odd rules that only seem to apply in the city.

I didn't fit into any of those categories.

I smiled as I stared out the window watching a trio of girls, all of them tall and skinny, all of them bedecked in black and walking on heels taller than anything I could possibly imagine myself walking in. They were laughing and talking as they walked along the street.

"What are you looking at? You're smiling." Dominick's voice drew my attention toward him.

"Just the city." I shrugged and went back to watching. "You've grown up here. Lived here all of your life. Unless you were traveling or..." Memory hit me though and I stopped, my throat locking up at me.

He reached out and took my hand, threading his

fingers between mine. "Don't. I don't want you freaking out over that. I just want to put it behind me. But I don't want it to be a wall between us, Aleena. Ever."

"Can you put it behind you?" I asked.

"Up until recently, I thought I had." He shrugged restlessly. "But I've just been fooling myself. I lie to myself and I find ways to cope, but that's not putting it behind me."

I scooted closer to him, which wasn't easy in my tight outfit. I curled up against him and rested my hand just above his heart.

"Maybe you're not supposed to put it behind you," I said gently. "Maybe what you're supposed to do is learn to live with it. Accept it. I'm not sure it's the same thing."

He didn't say anything.

"Have you..." I hesitated, but then forced myself to forge ahead. If we trusted each other, loved each other, we had to be able to talk about things, no matter how hard they were. "Have you talked to anybody about this? Counselors? Therapy?"

His laugh was bitter and ugly. "My mother had me in therapy until I thought I might kill myself just to stop it. It didn't help."

"What about survivors groups?"

He stiffened. "No." He shook his head and pulled our interlocked hands up so that he could press his lips against the back of my hand. "Look, I'm fine. I'm dealing." Then he laughed, better than before, but still not happy. "Listen to me. I'm lying. I know I am."

"You don't have to do anything you don't want to do, Dominic," I said. "But you've already said that you know you haven't put it behind you and that all you're doing is getting by. You deserve better than that. If there is a better way, you should try to find it."

***

Olympus was beyond anything I had ever imagined. I could definitely understand where they'd gotten the name. Home of the gods, indeed. If there had been a real Olympus, I figured they would have worn togas or whatever the garment of the day had been. Here it was suits and elegant gowns mingling with jeans and t-shirts.

And then there was the leather.

I had assumed I would see leather. Actually, I'd expected to see a lot more leather but when I did see it, it was enough to make the butterflies in my stomach take flight. It wasn't worn in the form of clothing, for the most part. It was more of an...accessory?

Like dog collars. And for the most part, that would be all the person was wearing. I suppressed the urge to put my hand to my neck. Dominic had given me a collar. Black velvet with little silver hoops that he used to attach various things. He'd explained to me the significance of asking me to wear it, that in the bdsm world, it would mean ownership. I'd been nervous that he'd ask me to wear it tonight, but he hadn't.

As we walked by a couple, my eyes lingered on the man. He was on his hands and knees, head bowed. Around his neck was a leather collar. The steel leash attached to it was being held by a strict-looking woman in a leather mini dress. When she paused to chat with a man in jeans and a t-shirt, the man on the leash leaned his head against her thigh. As I watched, she reached down and stroked his hair in an almost absent manner, as if she wasn't really even registering his presence.

The interaction sent a ripple of unease through me and I glanced up at Dominic. When we were out of earshot of the couple, I leaned towards him and spoke in a low voice. "The collar you gave me..." My stomach twisted. "I'll never do that."

He looked down at me, his lips curving into a soft smile. "The collar means you're mine, that no one else can approach you." He slid his hand from the small of my back to my hip, pulling me close to him. "I don't want that for us, but it makes them happy. They've been married for twenty years. To each their own."

We continued on for a few minutes before a woman in a red velvet corset and a long skinny black skirt stopped us. She leaned forward to kiss Dominic and he casually turned his head, catching the kiss on his cheek. His hand flexed on my hip, then slid around so that his fingers rested on my belly and I was tucked under his arm in a clearly possessive gesture.

"Natalie." He nodded at her and then turned his head toward me. "Aleena, this is an old friend of mine. Natalie, this is Aleena. My...girlfriend."

A thrill went through me at the word. We hadn't discussed what labels fit what we had, but I loved that he'd chosen something rather simplistic. In this world, the word lover didn't necessarily mean love. Girlfriend, however, meant that we were something outside of the bedroom.

Natalie's eyebrows went up. "Girlfriend?" She started to laugh, but stopped as she caught sight of the serious expression on Dominic's face. To my surprise, she turned to me and smiled, holding out her hand. "Aleena, is it? It's nice to meet you. Natalie Walsh."

At the table next to us, I heard the familiar sound of a hand striking flesh and a guttural moan. A man cried out and the muffled words, "Please mistress. I'm sorry. I didn't mean to displease..."

There was a second strike.

Blood rushed to my face and I was thankful for the dim lighting as I squeezed and shook Natalie's hand in return. "Aleena Davison."

"Let me guess," she said. The smile on her face was understanding. "Your first time."

I made a face. "Is it that obvious?"

She shrugged. "I say you're holding up rather well. You're not gawking and whipping your head around like a tourist."

"A tourist?"

"Dominic?" She glanced at him.

He looked at me and then shrugged. He led me

over to the railing. We had come in through what it seemed to be a private entrance, going straight up to the third level. Now we were staring down onto the bottom two levels. The upper levels were circular and open, so you could view the lower level and each floor was smaller, but narrower, almost like an old coliseum would have been laid out. The lowest level seemed to be almost like the entertainment for the upper levels. There was even a stage in the very center where it appeared someone was setting up for a show.

"Tourists," Natalie said from my other side. "They come for the shock of it, but they never stay for very long."

My breath caught as I realized several of the couples I'd thought were dancing were actually having sex, or something like it. I jerked my head up to stare at Dominic. He was watching me, clearly waiting to see how I would react. There was a wariness on his face and I knew what I did in the next few minutes would have an impact on our relationship. It was one thing to get kinky in the bedroom. It was something else entirely to be surrounded by it.

Slowly, I shifted my attention back to the dance floor. I couldn't hide my shock...or the arousal that was beginning to work its way through the surprise.

Bodies twisted. Twined. I watched as one woman went to her knees and presented her buttocks for a flogging. I squirmed and Dominic ran his hand up my ribcage, his fingertips caressing the side of my breast. I made a small sound but didn't look away from the floor.

There was a woman perched on the railing between the dance floor and the dining area and she had two people in front of her, a woman and a man. Each one was sucking on a nipple and she looked between the two with a patented, bored expression on her face. She held a cane in her hand and I watched as she used the cane to tap the man's cheek.

When he lifted his head, she nudged him back with the toe of one thigh-high, spike-heeled boot.

Another man took his place, wrapping his lips around the recently abandoned nipple.

"Auditioning," Dominic said in my ear. "She does that a lot. She's got a VIP membership and she can bring somebody up here with her, but she likes to play the new people. She won't bring anybody to the third floor. She never does."

The lights dimmed even more and I lost sight of the woman and the pair auditioning. I didn't try to look for them though as two people walked onto the stage.

It was a man. I squinted and realized I'd seen him earlier. The guy in jeans and t-shirt. He'd been talking to Natalie just before we'd come up to her. The woman with him wore a black silk cocktail dress and a mask.

He held rope.

Lots and lots of red rope.

As the crowd went silent, a low, melodic tune began to play. Weeping sax and rich violin, blended with the haunting strains from a piano. A pair of stage lights focused on the pair.

108

"What's going on?" I asked in a whisper.

"The show." Dominic leaned forward, his eyes narrowed. "Watch."

The man looked out at the audience and gave a slow smile.

And then he got to work.

***

I was dazed and sweating by the time it ended.

She wore a cage of ropes. I didn't have any other word for what I was seeing. The red ropes crisscrossed her body all the way down, breasts framed perfectly. Even her legs were caged, the *x*'ing pattern of the ropes continuing until she was immobilized, only her head, hands and feet left unbound. Her skin glistened with sweat and she stared with intense focus at the man as he bent down and kissed her gently.

"It's called shibari," Dominic said, his voice husky in my ear.

I jumped and then swallowed. I'd almost forgotten he was there. Now, I could feel his hand burning through the thin material of my shirt.

"Does that interest you?"

"Um..." I glanced at his face and saw he was smiling. Even in the dim light, I could see his eyes practically glow. "Yeah. It's well..." I struggled to find the right word. "Beautiful."

Hot.

I looked back at the stage just as the man picked up his partner and carried her off the stage, still bound.

"It was..." Words escaped me.

"Erotic."

No word had ever seemed more apt. "Yes."

When he took my hand, I let him lead me away. My legs were shaky, as if I'd been teased to the brink of something. I understood, to some extent, the bliss I'd seen on the woman's face although I realized some of what I was feeling was envy. I didn't quite understand it, but I wanted to.

Cool air brushed over me and I looked up, realized we were in a new room and we were alone.

My eyes shot to the bed, to the pole in the middle of the room, then the various instruments and devices left out for display. "Where are we?"

"One of the VIP rooms." Dominic turned to face me. He frowned as he brushed back some hair from my face. "What are you thinking?"

I bit my lip nervously. "I'm afraid you'll be upset."

"No." He rested his hands on my shoulders. "I want to know."

I could feel the tension in his hands, in his body. "I...the woman on the stage."

"His sub. I think they're permanent partners." Dominic's lashes lay low over his eyes, shielding his gaze from me. "Like us."

My chest tightened at that. Permanent. *Like us.*

He continued, "That sort of bondage takes a special degree of trust and training. If they aren't

110

partners, then she's been topped by somebody skilled in shibari before and he's studied it as well. It's an art form, one that takes practice on both sides." He gave me a curious look. "You want to try it."

"Well..." I was squirming now.

He cupped my face, not letting me look away. "What is it, Aleena?"

"It..." I blew out a breath. "Did you see her face? It was like she was somewhere else entirely. Only those two existed."

"For her, at that moment, it was just her and just him."

I still couldn't move my head, but I lowered my eyes. "I've felt that before. With us."

His fingers twitched on my cheeks.

"But it looked like...more. To be able to get that way with all those people..."

Dominic's voice was soft. "She gave herself over to him entirely. There was no doubt, not in him or in herself." He brushed his thumb across my bottom lip. "You've called me on holding back personally, but I think you've been holding back sexually."

I jerked my head up at that. "I...the things I've let you...I mean..."

His expression was serious. "That's what I mean. The things you've *let* me do to you? You're still ashamed of what you enjoy."

His word choice hit me. I'd accused him of being ashamed of me, but I'd never once considered that I was really the one ashamed. Not of him or of being with him. Not even of what we did, but rather the fact that I enjoyed it. All of it. I enjoyed him spanking me, using a flogger, restraining me. I loved the way he fucked me, the way he made love to me. How his cock felt in my pussy...in my ass.

"Aleena, darling."

His voice brought me back to him.

"Let go."

As I nodded, I felt as if something had broken free. Relief flooded through me. I didn't have to be ashamed of what I wanted, what I liked. I was safe with him.

He dropped his hands from my face, reaching down to lace his fingers between mine. "Now, be honest, do you want to be bound like that? It's something that has to be learned."

I thought about it, thought about how the ropes caught her breasts, ran between her thighs. I was tempted to say yes. "Do you know how?"

"No." He squeezed my hands. "Like I said, it's an art form. It takes practice. I know people who practice and it can be learned. I'll learn it, if that's something you want."

"I..." Blowing out a breath, I shook my head. "I don't think I'm ready for that."

He nodded. "We'll put it aside for now then." He let go of one of my hands and curled his hand around the back of my neck. "But I don't ever want you to feel like you have to be embarrassed to ask for something you want."

I smiled as I turned my head and kissed his wrist.

"Are you ready for something new though?"

I nodded and he turned me to face the pole, his body a hard, warm presence behind me.

"I do know my way around ropes, Aleena."

***

He hadn't lied.

He'd handcuffed me before, used various types of cloth to tie up my hands and legs. Nothing as elaborate as the shibari we'd witnessed on stage, but I knew the feel of restraints against my skin.

But this was different.

My hands were tied to the pole rather than to each other, the right just an inch above the left, with just enough give that I could hold on to the cool metal. When he'd done that, I'd thought that would be it, but it wasn't. He'd taken my left ankle and brought it up, tying it to my thigh, leaving me precariously perched on one foot. He wasn't finished even then. He pulled my left leg to the side, somehow fastening the rope to the pole in such a way that it left me exposed.

"You know the nice thing about the VIP rooms?" he asked as he finished checking my bonds.

I shook my head.

"They offer a selection of new tools, new toys, and anything I like, I can take home. There's a crop here I'm going to try on you, Aleena. Would you like that?"

"Yes, sir."

I gasped when he brought it down on my butt a moment later, sending a streak of pain through me. It was intense, a hot lick of flame up across my flesh. He repeated it, lower along my thigh, a lighter blow but still enough to burn. When he reached my ass again, he plied the crop with more force and I was whimpering by the time he stopped.

"What do you think? Should we keep it? Or try something else?"

Panting, I pressed my head to the pole. My ass felt like it was on fire. I could still feel each stroke.

"We'll try something else."

There was a pause, and then another type of pain. I heard the crack before I felt the heat bloom across my already sore ass. I cried out, my back arching as I fought my body's natural instinct to turn away.

"This is a paddle." He paused and came up behind me, stroking a hand up my back. "You remember your word, Aleena?"

"Please...Dominic, please..."

"Do you remember?" He demanded it now.

"Yes!"

"Good."

The next few minutes bled together, a hot miasma of pain, followed by a rush of relief that left me feeling like I was just going to drift away. He alternated between using the paddle on my ass and trading it out for the crop, which he used on my butt and thighs. Between my thighs. The first strike with the crop against my pussy sent me screaming into a nearly painful orgasm. As I came, I panted and begged for more in one breath, then in the next, I pleaded with him to stop.

He didn't though, timing his hits so that just as my climax was fading, he pushed me into another, this one even more intense than the last.

I wasn't sure at what point he released me, only that the ropes were gone and he was massaging my ankle and then my wrists as he held me up. Everything felt so surreal, but all that mattered was the stark, hungry look on his face.

He kissed me, hard, his tongue demanding as he plundered my mouth. His hands tightened around me until I knew I'd be bruised, but I didn't care. Then, suddenly, he was straightening, leading me somewhere. I barely registered that it was a table, only that he was bending me over it. The wood was cold against my hard nipples and I shivered.

"Hands," he ordered.

I obeyed and in short order, my hands were tied behind my back, forcing me to lay with my chest and cheek against the table.

"You've been a good girl, Aleena." His fingers brushed my hair out of my face. "I'm going to reward you now. Would you like that?"

"Yes, sir."

He buried himself inside me, no teasing, no warning. Just one hard, fast stroke. Even as I was still crying out from the sudden intrusion, he was pulling out and slamming forward again. He pounded into me, relentless, each stroke deeper than the last. The pressure inside me was building quickly, but as I tensed, my body ready for the next stroke to push me over the edge, he stopped.

He pulled out completely and I shuddered, trembling, clamping my thighs together against the ache of unfulfilled release. I felt so empty that I almost wanted to cry.

When he touched me again, I jumped. His fingers were cold.

"Relax, baby."

He slid his finger inside my ass and I gasped at the sharp burn. Biting my lip to keep back the whimpers, I tried to twist away. He brought down his hand on my left cheek and I made a pained sound, but I stopped trying to get away. When he added a second finger, I moaned but forced myself to take it. I closed my eyes, absorbing the sensations of his fingers twisting inside me, preparing me. I let the sound of his voice wash over me.

"That's it, baby. Just like that. Get ready to take my cock. So beautiful like this."

His hand caressed my ass and I shuddered. Between the paddle and the crop, my skin was so sensitive that the slightest touch made my nerves sing.

"Ready?"

I nodded, unable to speak.

When he started to push his cock inside me, I jerked against the ropes holding me and twisted, shuddering in need, shaking with mixed pain and pleasure. He kept his rhythm slow, working past the muscle, teasing it into relaxing. I whimpered as the pain tried to swallow me.

116

He spanked me three times in quick succession. When he did it a fourth time, I cried and twisted, forcing myself all the way back on him. He grunted as he filled me. I gasped.

He slid out and I tried to pull away, briefly wondering if I should use my safe word. No. I would trust him to know what I could take. I closed my eyes and completely gave myself over to him.

He fisted a hand in my hair and yanked, forcing my head back, my body bent at a nearly impossible angle. As he rode me, his free hand slid around to my breast and he took my nipple between his thumb and finger. He pinched and twisted and I came.

I screamed his name and I heard him swear even as I felt him come, his cock pulsing in my ass, throbbing in time with my own body.

***

Exhausted didn't even begin to cover how I felt. I couldn't even lift my head.

We were on the bed and I had no memory of getting here. My cheek was on Dominic's chest and I could hear the steady beating of his heart. I wanted to look at him, needed to see his face.

I tried to raise my head and groaned.

"Stop," he said, his hand pressing my head back down. "Your body needs rest."

"What the hell was that?" I mumbled.

"You got your first glimpse at what some people

call subspace."

I rolled my eyes up toward him.

He combed his fingers through my hair. It was a mess. I couldn't see it, but I knew. And I didn't care. The expression in his eyes was a lambent, happy one. Funny. A few weeks ago, I would have expected him to look smug after he practically screwed me into catatonia. Now, though, he just looked sated. Like a big cat.

"Subspace?"

"Hmmm." He shifted, bringing my body more upright. Then he rubbed his cheek against mine, again reminding me of a cat. "It's brought on by a rush of endorphins, adrenaline. Pain brings on endorphins and adrenaline. Then it drains away." He kissed the top of my head. "That's what happened on the stage."

Oh.

"You finally let yourself go completely." He sounded pleased...and happy. Genuinely happy.

I was glad he was happy and sure that if I thought about it, I'd be able to understand the whole subspace thing. If I could think. But I couldn't right then and I really didn't want to.

"Thinking's overrated," I announced, snuggling closer to him. He felt really, really good.

He might have laughed.

I didn't know and I didn't care.

I was so blissed out and happy, I didn't care about anything but staying right there.

Who knew that letting go could feel so good?

Chapter 10

Aleena

I popped a grape tomato in my mouth and hummed under my breath. "More of these," I told Francisco. "Whatever you're getting, it has to involve more of these."

He laughed. "I'll get more at the farmer's market tomorrow, okay?"

The doorbell rang but before I could get up to get it, I heard Dominic rising. He'd elected to work home today and I could tell Francisco had been amused by the two of us.

It had been a week since we'd gone to Olympus, a week of pure bliss. We'd fought through our demons and knew where we stood with each other. It was almost perfect.

Except for one thing that kept hovering in the background.

Rising from the chair, I moved over to the doorway and watched as Dominic ushered Kowalski in.

"We'll be in the office," Dominic said, his gaze

flicking toward the kitchen.

"Do you want me to bring in coffee or anything?" I asked.

Dominic glanced at the investigator, but the man just shook his head. He didn't have good news and my heart twisted painfully. I could almost feel Dominic's disappointment.

"No," he said. "We'll be fine."

As the two of them disappeared, I turned back to the kitchen and settled back down on the seat, forcing myself to smile as I looked at Francisco even though my thoughts were down the hall. We were quiet as Francisco jotted down a few notes and then passed them to me. I looked over the menu and shrugged, not as interested in food as I had been a few minutes ago.

"Miss Aleena."

"Aleena." I made a face. "Please. This *Miss Aleena* crap is so archaic."

Francisco chuckled, but there wasn't really any joy in it. "Archaic." He nodded slowly. "You know, I know of some *archaic* things that might interest you." His gaze flicked in the direction of the hall. "My family, for one. Do you know we've worked for the Snows for going on four generations now?"

"That's not...well, yeah, I guess it would be archaic." I tipped my glass of water toward him with a half-smile.

He chuckled and leaned back against the counter, arms crossed. "When you come from a family like mine, you grow up understanding certain rules. There are things that are done and things that aren't. One thing that is not done, is you do not talk about the family with outsiders."

He shrugged and studied his nails in a manner that was so patently nonchalant that it told me what he was saying was anything but casual.

"Now you might gossip with members of the staff, with those who work for other families even. But you will not chat with anybody outside the loop. Even years later." He smiled as he lifted his gaze to me. "It's just not done."

I narrowed my eyes as he glanced toward the office again. Okay? What was he trying to tell me?

"Unless, of course, somebody," he continued. "The right somebody, asked the right way."

"Francisco—"

"My grandfather worked for Mr. and Mrs. Snow back when they first brought Mr. Dominic home," he said, changing the subject so fast I almost got whiplash. He shoved off the counter and walked over to the refrigerator to check on supplies he'd already checked. "Grandfather talked about what a pretty baby he was. Fussy though. Sick and pretty small."

I slid off the stool and gripped the table, staring at the back of Francisco's averted head. Any other time, I would've been fascinated to hear about Dominic as a child, but I was focusing on the more important part of what Francisco had said. "Your grandfather?" My voice was level and calm.

"Yes." Mild eyes met mine and once more, he smiled. "He's retired now. Lives down near Atlantic City. Gambles a lot. Flirts with women. I go see him every other weekend. He'd talk a man's ear off. He called me last night, told me about a visitor he had. A skinny man with glasses. Grandfather couldn't wait to remind me about all those rules a family like mine has, Miss Aleena." He sighed then and shook his head. "He always did like Mr. Dominic though."

I jumped off the stool and walked to the office as fast as I could without actually running. Both men turned to look at me when I burst through the doors.

"Did you go and see..." I wracked my head for Francisco's last name and couldn't think of it. Growling in frustration, I looked at Dominic. "Francisco's grandfather. You know him?"

Confused, Dominic stood up. "Yeah. Antonio." He sucked in a breath, his eyes widening. "Is something—?"

"He's fine." I made a dismissive motion and pointed at Kowalski. "Did you talk to an old guy named Antonio?"

Kowalski rocked back on his heels, tucking his hands into the pockets of a pair of worn, faded corduroys. His expression gave nothing away. "It's possible I did. I'm afraid I haven't learned much, though. I—"

"They aren't going to tell *you* anything." I walked across the room and grabbed Dominic's hand. "Come on!"

He stared at me, still clearly confused, but he let me pull him up. He followed me out, Kowalski trailing along behind us.

Francisco was waiting for us in the living room, seated.

There was a neat tray of hors d'oeuvres on the table. Nothing fancy, but the man did work fast. He folded his hands and met Dominic's gaze as he lowered himself to the couch, eying the chef narrowly.

"Just what is this?" Dominic asked.

Francisco looked at me and I nodded.

"Mr. Dominic," Francisco said softly. "I think you should talk to my grandfather. *You,* not an investigator."

"About what?" Dominic's voice was flat and hard and I saw the flicker of anger in his eyes. I knew how much he valued his privacy.

Before Francisco had to explain, I laid a hand on Dominic's thigh. "He talks to his grandfather all the time, baby. Kowalski was just out there and Francisco talked to Antonio last night. What do you think you should talk to him about?"

Dominic looked over at Kowalski.

Francisco bowed his head, but not before I caught a glimpse of his face. He had known before.

"Why do I need to talk to Antonio?" Dominic said quietly.

"Because he knows things that he isn't going to tell somebody outside the family," Francisco said softly. "I don't know if he has answers, but he could point you the right direction."

Chapter 11

Dominic

Antonio Salvatore had the wrinkled, leathery skin of a man who'd seen a lot of years. He also had the wide, easy smile of a man who'd spent a lot of those years laughing.

As he sat rocking on the chair, he looked at me with eyes that held no hint of the laughter though.

"Some bad things were happening about that time, Dominic." He nodded and went back to staring out over the waters of the Atlantic. "Lots of bad things. A few of us..." He paused and looked back at me. "Us workers, you see. Some of us thought something was wrong. One girl, she went to the police. She went to boarding school in France and ended up getting sent back. She had a little girl, lived with a boy she'd met from Brooklyn. But only for a short while, then suddenly, she was back in school. The boy from Brooklyn was gone and her daughter...I don't know if she ever saw her daughter again. Made a lot of people afraid to say anything."

Aleena put her hand on my knee, but I barely felt it.

Antonio continued, "I always figured they had some cops involved to help smooth things over. People like us, people see through us, and so we see a lot."

"What happened?" I asked. "Antonio, what do you know?"

"Nothing for sure." He shrugged and went back to staring out over the water. "It all ended a few years after they adopted you."

"Was there anything going on when I was adopted?" My voice was even, a miracle.

Antonio pressed his lips flat. "I don't like to do this. I really don't."

"Antonio—"

The old man turned, reaching for a book he had on the table next to his chair. Inside it was a folded up sheet of paper. He handed it to me without a word.

I unfolded it and stared, confused. The picture was of a young woman. Attractive, with sharp features and intelligent eyes. "What..."

"Her name is Cecily Cole." Antonio looked at me as I raised my head.

Shit.

Cecily Cole was a name both feared and worshipped among the social circuit. An heiress, she'd lived and partied hard as a teen, taking herself to the brink of total disaster. Now she was a crusader of sorts, and she scorned New York society with a zeal that made them almost slavishly devoted.

126

"Is she involved in...whatever this was?" Considering her prominence, I hoped not.

"You could say that," Antonio said. "She got into drugs when she was young. Twelve or thirteen, I've heard talk. Ended up living the wild life. When she was nineteen, she was found in a compromising position with a U.S. senator and ended up pregnant. Naturally, it was all her fault—that nineteen year-old troubled girl." He let his voice clearly say how he felt about that blame.

My skin went cold and I shook my head. "What..."

"My sister was her nana. Took care of her from the time she was a baby. Was there the night she went into labor. They let her stay with Cecily, because it calmed the girl, you know. But the next day, she was given her walking papers...she'd hoped they'd let her stay and take care of the baby. But they told her the baby was being put up for adoption."

I swallowed, hard and fast. "Okay. So...she put me up—"

"No." Antonio opened the book on the table and handed it to me, pointing at a paragraph at the top of the left page.

—The day I lost my baby was the day I knew I had to turn my life around. He died in my womb. I never got to hold him. Never got to see him. I never even got to hear him cry, because he was born lifeless, thanks to the abuse I'd heaped on my body over the years.

I grabbed the book and read that paragraph, over and over.

Finally I hurled it against the wall and surged upright. Aleena went to catch my hand, but I shook her off. I didn't want to be touched at the moment. Wheeling around, I stared out over the water, but it did nothing to calm me.

Nothing.

I turned back to Antonio. "What's all this about? Do you know anything or not?"

"My sister, Isabel, was in that room when Cecily's baby was born. A private doctor was brought in and Cecily was sedated, heavily. Then a C-section performed. A healthy, *living* baby boy was delivered, Dominic. My sister was there."

He gestured at the book. "Isabel is dead now, a heart attack, just a year before that book was released. But my sister wouldn't have confused a living, crying baby boy with a stillborn."

"Dominic..."

Dazed, I looked over at Aleena. She had her tablet out, but I didn't want to see whatever it was. I just wanted to take off, walk. Do something. Anything to empty my head.

"Dominic!" She walked over to me and shoved the iPad into my hands. "Cecily names the senator she slept with. Look at his picture!"

I looked down.

Then staggered back.

His hair was brown, unlike mine, but other than that, we might as well have been made from the same mold.

"He..."

I cleared my throat. Okay, so if that was the guy who got Cecily Cole pregnant...

I looked back at the picture I held in my hands.

"Is she my mother?"

Chapter 12

Aleena

When we left Antonio's, Dominic asked me to drive. We hadn't wanted anyone to know what we were doing so we hadn't had one of the drivers take us. I was beginning to wish we had.

Dominic sat rigid and unyielding in his seat for the first five minutes before reaching into the interior pocket of his suit and pulling out a phone. He was so quiet, so closed off.

I'd never been so worried about him. I didn't know what to do, what to say. The first ten minutes or so stretched out without me saying anything.

He was actually the first one to speak, gesturing toward the exit for Philadelphia. "Take that one."

"Ah...aren't we going home?" Confused, I shot him a quick look before changing lanes. Several horns blared and I clenched my teeth as I forced my way through another lane of traffic. I was once again reminded why I didn't want to drive in New York

City. Jersey was bad enough.

"We'll need gas soon. Once we fill up, I'll take over driving." He spoke in a neutral, business-like voice, the way he'd talk to a stranger.

I just nodded and took the exit. Once the attendant had finished pumping the gas, we traded out, Dominic taking over the driver's seat as I slid into the passenger side. My concern for him grew as we drove on in silence.

Finally, I asked, "Where are we going?"

Dominic just shook his head.

Normally, time with Dominic moved by too fast, but these minutes dragged out indefinitely. He didn't speak. He hardly moved, other than what was needed to drive.

It was unsettling and it occurred to me how used I was to seeing him move. Or having him touch me. The brush of his hand on my cheek, or even just resting it on my knee, but he was on lockdown now, sitting behind the wheel, jaw clenched and shoulders tight. I thought the lightest touch would make him shatter.

Or explode.

"Do you want to talk about this?" I asked him softly.

"No."

I tried not to let the sharp word hurt. "Okay. When you're ready, I'll listen."

I looked out the window, watching as we rolled into Philadelphia. The city was still unfamiliar to me. I'd only been there a couple of times now, but it was a nice city. I liked the history of it and it was a

132

friendly enough place. It wasn't home, but I liked it.

Clearing my throat, I said, "I can find out information on Cecily Cole. See if we can figure out how to set up a meeting between the two of you. I'm—"

The words came to an abrupt halt in my throat as he pulled the car up in front of a hotel. It was an elegant, glamorous sprawl of metal and glass, a familiar one. Masque Philadelphia. The hotel we stayed at when we'd gone to Philadelphia not long ago when he had been looking to take over *Devoted*. Dominic's hotel.

"What are we doing here?"

Dominic didn't say anything. He climbed out and tossed his keys to the valet who greeted him by name. Again, no response. As he strode inside, I trotted after him to catch up. Then I crashed into him, because he'd come to an abrupt halt, just inside the doors.

He was staring at a massive banner, draping down into the open-air atrium from several stories up. The banner was huge, taking up two full levels. It was completely dominated on one side by a woman's face.

On the other side, there was a symbol. I only recognized it because I'd seen it earlier, when I'd done my quick search on her back at Antonio's place. Overlying the symbol were the words: *Our children are our future. We owe them better.*

Cecily Cole was a striking woman. I could see that as I gazed up at her enlarged image.

Suddenly, the pit of my stomach dropped out as

I realized what was going on. She was an activist and a philanthropist. This was some sort of gala, probably a fundraiser for one of the youth charities she either ran or endorsed. Judging by the people gathered around us or lining up near the escalators to go down a level toward the ballroom, this looked to be some sort of formal affair too.

I might have started to laugh hysterically if I had the chance, or the time, but I already knew what would happen. This fancy party of hers was about to be crashed...by her son. The one she thought had died at birth. What a crazy twist of fate had brought her here, to her son's hotel.

Security wouldn't throw him out. Not Dominic Snow.

I mentally groaned as I heard somebody greeting him, and me, from several feet away. "Mr. Snow! Ms. Davison...I didn't know we were expecting you today..."

His voice got lost in the rush of noise as Dominic started to move forward, focused on nothing but the image of the woman staring down at him from two stories over our heads.

Our children...

That had to hurt so much.

I shot a look at the woman I recognized from the concierge staff and shook my head, then I rushed after Dominic.

"Stop." I caught his arm and squeezed gently.

"Let go."

I'd heard that tone of voice before, but never directed at me. I pushed aside the stab of hurt. I couldn't imagine how much pain he was in. I couldn't imagine how he was feeling, but in my heart, I knew this wasn't the way. He had to want to know his mother and I couldn't imagine her not wanting to know him. But he couldn't do it this way.

As he tried to shake me off, I tightened my grip. "Not like *this*."

"I'm going to see her. I have that right." He didn't even look at me.

"You aren't wrong. I'm not arguing that." I squeezed his arm again and stepped in front of him. I put my hand on his cheek. "But look around you, baby. *Look*."

His jaw flexed as he finally looked down at me.

"What do you think she's doing? *Who* do you think she's doing this *for*?"

Some of the steel left his spine and I heard a ragged intake of breath. I dared to move in closer, dared to let go of his arm and take his hand. "This is all about *you*. She turned her entire life around because of you, to make up for what she thought she had done to *you*. She blamed herself for you dying when you were really stolen away. Neither of you are to blame for that, but all of this...she's done so much good and it was all because of you."

He was staring at the floor now, shoulders rising and falling raggedly. "Aleena..."

The pain in his voice made me wince. "Let her do what she came here for. We'll find her. You'll talk to her. But don't just crash in there like this. Yeah, you deserve to know her, but she's spent her life missing you. You're going to knock her off her feet

135

when you do this. Don't do it in a room full of strangers."

***

Dominic and I ended up in the executive offices normally used by the hotel manager. In news that surprised me not at all, there were no rooms open at the Masque. The hotel manager apologized effusively, so much so that I felt bad for him and tried to assure him that he didn't need to worry about it.

As he backed out of the office, amidst his third apology, he promised to send up dinner and a bottle of Dominic's favorite scotch.

"Could I possibly offer anything else?" he asked, hesitating.

"Ah...a dress? Something black and formal?" I asked, looking down at myself. "Fast?" I looked at my beige heels and made a face. "Shoes too?"

He peered at my feet, then ran his gaze up and down my body. There was no lust there, only a practiced eye. With a smile, he accurately guessed the sizes I'd need. "Give me thirty minutes, Ms. Davison." He flicked a look at Dominic's averted back. I shook my head.

He nodded and left without another word.

"You flustered him," I said.

Dominic didn't respond. I moved toward him, uncertain if I should, but needing to touch him, to

136

try to offer some sort of reassurance. Even as I was lifting a hand, he turned, catching me in his arms. He pulled me tight against his body and his mouth came down on mine, hard and demanding. I clung to him as he kissed me, as his teeth sunk into my bottom lip hard enough to make me gasp.

He tore his mouth from mine. "Make me stop thinking, please. Even for just a few minutes."

"Whatever you need." I glanced behind me. "The door..."

He let go, his fingers lingering at my waist for a moment. I hurried over to turn the lock and when I turned around, he was there, his pants already undone, his cock thick and hard.

His eyes burning into me, he backed me up against the solid oak of the door and reached down, dragging my skirt up around my waist. He lifted me, one arm bracing me against the door, the other moving between us to pull aside the crotch of my panties.

"I'm sorry. I can't...I have to be inside you," he said, his voice raw. He stared at me with broken eyes and I put my hand on his cheek.

"Whatever you need."

He thrust inside me and I swallowed a cry. I wasn't ready for him and I bit my lip as he began a slow, devastating invasion. His cock rasped against folds just barely wet and then he withdrew. He surged in a little deeper and I took him better because I was wetter now, but not enough. Then he started all over again.

It was intimate and raw and powerful and I

clung to him, whispering small, meaningless words as I encouraged him to take solace in my body. His mouth ate at mine, his teeth nipping my lower lip, his tongue thrusting deep and echoing the rhythm of his body.

There was a knock at the door.

"Mr. Snow. I have—"

I moaned.

"Ah...Mr. Snow?"

"Leave it outside the door."

Dominic's voice was harsh and I had no doubt the manager knew exactly what we were doing. But I didn't care. I had nothing to be ashamed of. The man I loved was hurting and I was comforting him. There was no shame in that.

Dominic slammed into me harder, his eyes as dark as a night sky. "I love you," he said. His fingers twisted in my hair and he dragged my mouth back to his. "Tell me you love me."

"I love you." I bit his lip, felt him stiffen, felt his cock swell. "You know I do. I love you. I want you." I twisted my fingers in the hair at the base of his skull. "You're mine."

He groaned, then, started to come.

I wasn't there yet and I writhed against him, desperate, but he was there, taking care of me. He pushed his hand between us, stroked my clit in quick, hard strokes.

I whimpered and jerked against him as he shoved straight up in me, impaling me on his cock as he emptied himself inside me. And then I was right there with him.

When we opened the door, I had a neat, black formal waiting for me, along with a pair of elegant heels with sparkly little straps that winked in the light. The dress was simple. It clung to my curves and fell straight to the floor. I had no jewelry and had to rush through washing up in the bathroom, but it would have to be enough. I knew Dominic wouldn't be content to wait for long, but once I dressed, I'd told him to trust me. I asked him to give me thirty minutes to go out and try to make this go as smooth as possible.

I guess he knew the same thing I did—if he kept staring up at the massive banner, he wouldn't be able to wait, so he stayed in the office as I slipped out, leaving him to sip on his scotch and stare at the food neither of us had been able to eat.

As I made my way into the main lobby, I mentally prepared myself for what I might say and how I could make this happen. If positions were reversed, and somebody was trying to get to Dominic. How would they make that happen? Through me, I realized. That meant I needed to find Cecily Cole's people. Her assistant, secretary, PA, whatever term she used, whomever she had with her.

Plan of action set, I scanned the crowd. One of the gala organizers caught sight of me and started to hustle my way. Clearly, my quick clean up wasn't passing muster. A moment later, I was about ready to kiss the hotel manager, because a member of hotel security cut the woman off and spoke to her quietly. She gave me a disgruntled look, but walked off. I smiled at the security guard, looking professional and competent in his black suit. He tipped an imaginary hat at me and resumed his post.

I was about ready to whip out my phone and do a Google search—*who is Cicely Cole's personal assistant*—when I caught sight of a small, but heated discussion taking place near the main doors.

It was quieter out in the lobby now. I could hear a dull roar coming from inside the ballroom, which meant the party was probably revving up. A trim, elegant woman with snow white hair and razor-sharp cheekbones was speaking to a stocky, squarely built man in a discreet suit.

I studied him for a long moment and then looked at the woman. She bore a striking resemblance to Cecily. The cheekbones, the facial structure in general, although this woman looked as though she never smiled. There was an older gentleman with her who looked...faded. Graying, tired and weak, like there wasn't much of him left.

They faced the square, solid man with an air of indignation. He smiled politely back at them and shook his head.

Bingo.

I glided closer, accepted a glass of champagne from a strolling waiter when it was offered. The better to blend in, of course. Taking the edge off was just a bonus. When the older couple moved off, I moved in and held out my hand.

"Hello. I'm Aleena Davison...I'm Dominic Snow's personal assistant."

He glanced at me and then smiled. "Ms. Davison. I'm Tom, Cecily's assistant. I hadn't heard Mr. Snow would be in attendance at the gala tonight. Ms. Cole would be delighted to speak with him." His smile widened into an all-out grin. "I'll warn you, she is priming the guests for donations as we speak."

"Yes, well..." *Here goes nothing.* "He's actually not down as a guest. He does want to speak with her though."

Don't be mad at me, Dominic. I sweetened the pot. "If you can coax her into giving him some one-on-one time this evening, I can promise you he'll sign a check. Dominic is very much a believer in Ms. Cole's cause."

Tom's eyes were thoughtful. After a moment, he nodded slowly. "I can talk with her, see if we can work something out. Might I ask what it's in regards to?"

"Well, that's more his concern than mine." I gave him an easy smile and shrugged. "You know how it is, right?"

***

"A believer in her cause?" Dominic raised an eyebrow.

I gave him a weak smile. "I wanted to make sure she'd come up here." With a wince, I said, "Do I

141

need to apologize?"

"No." He looked up from the empty glass he'd been studying and gave me a bleak smile. "You did exactly what you'd promised, Aleena. And hell, it's not a bad cause."

Then he sighed and went back to staring into his drink.

I settled down next to him and looked at the clock. "Tom told me he'd get back to me about a time. I don't have any idea when it will be."

Dominic pulled me onto his lap and I settled my head on his shoulder.

"I can think of several ways to pass the time," he whispered into my ear, his fingers teasing my thigh through the slit in my skirt.

I reluctantly shook my head. "No." Despite the fact that my pussy was still throbbing from his prior rough treatment, my body protested my refusal. "If he says twenty minutes from now, I'm not going to pull open that door looking like...like..."

"Like the woman I'm desperate to touch?" He ran his fingers down my cheek. "To make love to? All the time? Every day? Every way I can?"

I slid my eyes to meet his and leaned in, kissing him firmly. "Stop being a living, breathing temptation."

He kissed me back with more enthusiasm, his tongue sliding into my mouth for a slow, pleasurable exploration. He sighed as he finally broke the kiss and then repositioned me so that we were sitting side by side.

"Fine. We'll watch a movie instead."

142

He didn't sound enthusiastic.
Neither was I.
Waiting sucked.

Chapter 13

Dominic

The movie played on, but neither of us paid much attention. It was a mutual favorite, but we couldn't focus on much of anything. Every couple of minutes, I'd look at the clock. Then she would. I was definitely wishing I could've talked Aleena into occupying me with her mouth, her body...

Fuck. I understood why she hadn't wanted to though. She cared what...Ms. Cole thought about her.

As the movie ended, the minute hand swept up to twelve, while the hour hand brushed eleven.

"Late hour for a meeting," Aleena said, trying to break the silence. She smiled at me.

I reached up and touched her cheek. "I love you." I could hardly believe how easily the words came now.

She covered my hand with hers and nodded. Then she stood up and turned off the TV. I watched her, elegant and sleek in black velvet, as she moved across the floor. I got up and went to pour myself a drink. It was my third and I was pushing it, but I didn't much care at that point.

The knock came just as I was tossing back half the scotch. I choked, the fiery liquid burning a path between throat and lungs.

Aleena shot me a look as she hurried to answer. I turned away, struggled to regulate my breathing. Fuck. Oh, fuck.

"Hello, Tom. Ms. Cole..."

Ms. Cole. My mother...

Dimly, I heard her speaking. I swiped the back of my hand over my mouth, sucked in a breath and tried to steady myself.

"Ms. Davison, hello. Tom tells me your Mr. Snow has a proposition..."

I turned.

Her gaze came to me and then started to move away.

It snapped back almost immediately and I watched as she lapsed into silence, her face going pale. Shit. I'd forgotten how much I looked like *him*, the senator. The man who'd gotten her pregnant. My father. Shit.

I didn't know what to say. Dammit. Why hadn't I thought of something to say, how to say this?

Her face was ghost white, eyes huge and startled.

"Ms. Cole. May I offer you a seat?" Aleena touched her arm. Cecily looked around, dazed and then nodded, letting Aleena guide her to a couch.

Tom was staring at me, hard, dislike clear in his

146

eyes. He'd already figured out that something wasn't quite right here.

I swallowed and reached up to tug at a tie I wasn't even wearing. I just couldn't breathe.

Aleena looked at me and I stared at her helplessly. I didn't know what to do. What to say. Me, Dominic Snow, who was always in control, was completely at a loss.

Aleena gave me an encouraging smile and then looked back at Cecily. "Ms. Cole. I..." She paused and then said, "I need to beg your understanding and your patience. Please."

Cecily was still staring at me.

"Ms. Cole?"

Finally, she looked at Aleena and nodded.

I retreated back behind the desk and listened. Listened as the woman I'd never expected to love told the woman I'd never expected to find a story that sounded insane, even to me. But it had nothing to do with me. It was about the baby snatching ring from twenty years ago. When she stopped, Cecily was twisting a handkerchief around and around in her hands. After a moment, she looked up. "I know all about that ring, Ms. Davison." She hesitated and then said, "I assume you're telling me this because you know about my son."

"Yes."

Cecily nodded and struggled to smile. It was an attempt at a cool, collected smile and it was a damn good one.

But it wobbled and I could see the bleak heartbreak in her eyes. What were we doing? I didn't need to know that badly. I didn't need to tear open old wounds, did I? What kind of person was I that I'd hurt this kind, caring woman?

"If you know about him, then you know that my son died twenty-eight years ago. A doctor was there. He pronounced him dead at birth."

Aleena leaned forward. The compassion that had gotten to me from the beginning showed in her eyes. "Your nana heard him crying."

For a long moment, Cecily just stared at her. Then she leapt up, her jaw going tight. "No!" Her voice was harsh, jagged. Fists clenched at her sides. "No. Stop this. You...why are you doing this? It's cruel. Isabel left because of what I'd done. Because I'd *killed* my son with the life I lived." She swept the room with a gaze, but this time, her eyes bounced right off me as though I wasn't there. "Tom, we're leaving."

But Tom was studying me, and it wasn't dislike in his eyes anymore. It was something else.

"She *heard* him crying, Ms. Cole," Aleena said again, her voice gentle. "We spoke to her brother. She was fired the day after you gave birth. She didn't want to leave. They made her. They wouldn't let her come back, Cecily. They fired her because she knew you'd given birth to a healthy boy and they sold him."

"No." It was a whisper this time.

Her eyes skipped to me, held for a bare moment and I knew she was seeing the face of the man who'd fathered me. She'd felt something for him, I realized with a start. I could see it in her eyes. He'd turned

148

his back on her. She'd written that much in the book. She'd thought she loved him and now she was staring at a man who looked so much like him.

Clearing my throat, I said, "My name is Dominic Snow."

She jerked at the sound of my voice, as though it hurt.

"Twenty-eight years ago, on April twenty-seventh, my parents brought me home. I'm adopted..."

I stood up and walked over to her. She sat back down onto the couch, staring up at me with guarded eyes.

I settled on the chair across from hers, not wanting to spook her by sitting closer. "What day was your son born?"

"April twenty-sixth." Her eye sketched a quick, nervous circle across my face.

"The private investigator I hired made some loose connections between the people who facilitated my adoption and a lawyer your parents used. There was a...sizable transaction that week." Five hundred thousand dollars. The cost of a healthy baby boy.

She flinched as though she'd been slapped.

"They said he died." She said it pleadingly, in the voice of the child she once was. But she didn't sound like she believed it anymore.

I looked down, bracing myself. Then, slowly, I slid off the chair and settled on my knees a foot away from her. "I'm just about positive they lied, Ms. Cole."

She took a deep breath and then reached up and touched my cheek. "So...my son's name is Dominic."

Chapter 14

Aleena

It had been three days. The first twenty-four hours had been a whirlwind of paternity testing and questions. The testing had been gently suggested by Tom. "You would both feel better, knowing for sure," he'd said.

He was likely right, though I was grateful I hadn't needed to suggest it.

The tests, done on a rush in under twelve hours, were positive. Cecily Cole was Dominic's mother.

The FBI was brought in directly since the case had originally gone to them when it had first been uncovered. With the new information, and two new players—namely the elderly couple I'd seen Tom speaking with—the authorities were confident they could start finding some of the bigger names, and possibly track down other stolen babies.

I almost felt sorry for the Coles. They had only done what they'd thought was necessary to protect their family's reputation. Now, Cecily was cutting off

151

what little contact she'd kept with them and they'd never get to know the wonderful man their grandson had become. Still, the 'almost' was all there was. Seeing how badly they'd hurt Cecily took away most of the sympathy I would've had.

Dominic's parents were a different matter legally. They'd thought they were participating in a private adoption, a pricy one, but a legit one. Or at least one with the mother's consent. Even the FBI said the papers looked legitimate. If Dominic's mother had had some reservations, something her hunger for a baby had made her overlook...well, it wasn't anything she would be convicted of. Despite her flaws, in some ways she was a victim too. And now, she had to look at Dominic and Cecily for the rest of her life and know how she'd hurt them both.

The worst part of the whole thing was the press. Someone along the way had leaked the news and we'd been swarmed as soon as we'd gotten back to New York. We'd retreated to the house in the Hamptons for some quiet and now, as night fell, Dominic and I sat staring out over the ocean and listening to the cry of the gulls.

"You won't be staying in the guest house anymore," Dominic said suddenly, breaking the silence.

I rested my head against his chest, smiled. "Yes, sir."

His lips brushed my neck. "I love hearing you say that," he murmured.

"I love you." I turned my face and whispered the words against his cheek.

He turned his head so that our foreheads touched. "I love you." He hooked his finger around my necklace. "Did you ever think that this necklace would come in so handy?"

"How so?"

"Well, it brought us together, didn't it?"

I laughed. "That's a good point."

His fingers slid along the chain then lower, the tip of one teasing the neckline of my shirt. "Come here."

I shivered and glanced around us, recognizing the tone in his voice.

"There's nobody here." Clearly tired of waiting, he pulled me into his lap. His hands slid up under the hem of my skirt, the heat of his hands sending a shiver up my spine. I'd never lounged around in a skirt before I'd met him, but I was definitely learning the appeal of easy access.

I looped my arms around his neck as he bent forward, arching me backward. He pressed a hot, openmouthed kiss to the center of my chest, his mouth open. It was a raw, intimate touch, so much more than a kiss, so much more than a caress.

One arm remained at my back, steadying me, while the other went between us. I could feel him working at his trousers, then tugging my panties aside.

"Inside...?" I whispered.

"Yes. Inside you. Here. Now."

The demand in his voice was enough to make me not care that we were outside. I groaned as, mere seconds later, he fulfilled that promise, shoving inside me. I was wet and eager; he was hard, demanding, our bodies moving together in perfect sync.

"Take off your shirt," he said, his fingers digging into my hips as he lifted me, then brought me down, guiding me into a hard, driving rhythm.

My fingers skipped along the row of buttons, shaking, fumbling. When I reached the last one, he took over, shoving the shirt down until it trapped my arms at my elbows. Then he reached for my bra, freeing the clasp and shoving the cups open. "I love your tits," he muttered, cupping them in his hands as he continued to rock up, driving into me. He slumped deeper onto the couch, rolling my nipples between thumb and forefinger. "Ride me, Aleena. I want to see you, watch you." His hips stopped. "Use me to make yourself come."

I swallowed and stared down at him, unfamiliar with this. He was always the one in control. A faint smile curled his lips, as though he knew exactly what I was thinking.

"Ride me," he said again, one hand going to my hip and showing me the rhythm.

Slowly, I started to move. Up. Down. He cupped my breasts, teased my nipples, but his hips stayed still. I looked down, staring at his hands on my breasts. His cock swelled inside me and I cried out, leaning forward. It changed everything, the angle of his cock, how it felt inside me.

"That's it, baby...ride me..."

I moved faster, felt everything clenching inside me. Unable to stay still any longer, he started to thrust up, meeting my every downward stroke.

Too much, too much—

I threw back my head and cried out his name.

He moaned mine.

We climaxed together, bodies shuddering as we moved against each other, drawing out every last drop of pleasure until we couldn't hold anymore.

As I slumped against his chest, he slid one hand up my back, under the tangle we'd made of my shirt. I shuddered as his cock twitched inside me, sending a series of sensation tripping through me.

He sighed and shifted, rolling so that we lay sideways on the fat, well-padded cushions of the outdoor couch. Tucking my head into the nook just below his chin, I smiled. "I was thinking..."

"Thinking..." Dominic rubbed his cheek against mine. "If you were thinking just now, I may have to deal with a damaged ego."

I laughed and pressed a kiss against his side. "No. But...well, my necklace, yeah. It broke. But maybe I should send my old boss a thank you note. If he hadn't decided to be such an ass, you might not have felt the need to come rushing to my rescue. Who knows...we might not be here. And I'm pretty happy being right here."

"Oh, Aleena." He wrapped me up tight, hugging me closer. So close I could barely breathe. "I would have found you. I was all but waiting for a reason to hunt you down. I just didn't realize it."

The End

We hope you enjoyed Serving HIM as much as we enjoyed writing it. We can't get enough of Aleena and Dominic and we feel there is so much more to tell about their story. Therefore, we have decided to write a follow-up. Get ready for Craving HIM, coming in late August

Until then we are very excited to tell you about our next collaboration, PURE LUST, a six book series, coming in July/August.

There's also exciting news about M. S. Parker's latest series, Exotic Desires. All three books are now in Kindle Unlimited.

Acknowledgement

First, we would like to thank all of our readers. Without you, our books would not exist. We truly appreciate each and every one of you.

A big "thanks" goes out to all the Facebook fans, street team, beta readers, and advanced reviewers. You are a HUGE part of the success of the series.

We have to thank our PA, Shannon Hunt. Without you our lives would be a complete and utter mess. Also a big thank you goes out to our editor Lynette and our wonderful cover designer, Sinisa. You make our ideas and writing look so good.

About The Authors

MS Parker

M. S. Parker is a USA Today Bestselling author and the author of the Erotic Romance series, Club Privè and Chasing Perfection.

Living in Southern California, she enjoys sitting by the pool with her laptop writing on her next spicy romance.

Growing up all she wanted to be was a dancer, actor or author. So far only the latter has come true but M. S. Parker hasn't retired her dancing shoes just yet. She is still waiting for the call for her to appear on Dancing With The Stars.

When M. S. isn't writing, she can usually be found reading– oops, scratch that! She is always writing.

Cassie Wild

Cassie Wild loves romance. Every since she was eight years old she's been reading every romance novel she could get her hands on, always dreaming of writing her own romance novels.

When MS Parker approached her about co-authoring the Serving HIM series, it didn't take Cassie many seconds to say a big yes!!

Serving HIM is only the beginning to the collaboration between MS Parker and Cassie Wild. Another series is already in the planning stages.

42525537R00092

Made in the USA
Lexington, KY
17 June 2019